He was a father.

And now he was at the kitchen sink washing his son's hands, when Maggie shouted, "Flint! Come here."

He heard the trepidation in her voice. With the child tucked behind him, Flint led the way into the boy's bedroom, where Maggie paced. "What's wrong?"

"The window."

Flint bent to peer at it. "It looks okay."

She pointed with a shaky finger. "The glass does. The screen is missing."

"Maybe it just fell out. This is an old house."

"Yes, it is," Maggie replied. "And the screens are so warped they're nailed in."

"Somebody pulled nails out to get it off?" His heart started pounding so hard it felt as if it might go through his chest. "We should call the sheriff."

"Not again. I keep calling and pretty soon they won't make a run out here, let alone in a hurry. I think that's part of the stalker's plan."

"That's paranoid, Maggie."

"Only if nobody's after me."

Flint nodded. "Us. After us."

And now they were after their son.

Valerie Hansen was thirty when she awoke to the presence of the Lord in her life and turned to Jesus. She now lives in a renovated farmhouse in the breathtakingly beautiful Ozark Mountains of Arkansas and is privileged to share her personal faith by telling the stories of her heart for Love Inspired. Life doesn't get much better than that!

Books by Valerie Hansen

Love Inspired Suspense

Serenity, Arkansas

The Defenders

Capitol K-9 Unit

Visit the Author Profile page at Harlequin.com for more titles.

DANGEROUS LEGACY

VALERIE HANSEN

HARLEQUIN® LOVE INSPIRED® SUSPENSE

Recycling programs for this product may not exist in your area.

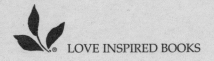 LOVE INSPIRED BOOKS

ISBN-13: 978-0-373-67762-7

Dangerous Legacy

Copyright © 2016 by Valerie Whisenand

www.Harlequin.com

Printed in U.S.A.

"A good man out of the good treasure
of his heart brings forth good;
an evil man out of the evil treasure
of his heart brings forth evil."
—Luke 6:45

To my Joe, who will always be looking over my shoulder as I write. He was an extraordinary gift from God.

ONE

"I didn't expect this kind of assignment so soon." Flint Crawford raked his fingers through his wavy golden hair and faced his captain. "I just got here. Can't you at least give me time to get settled?"

The older Arkansas Game and Fish officer was frowning. "Sorry. No. None of my other wardens have been able to get close to locating this bunch of poachers. Your connection with the Morgan woman is invaluable."

"She hates me," Flint argued.

"Doesn't matter. At least she knows you personally. Use that to our advantage. Get back in her good graces and find out where her uncle Elwood is hiding." Captain Lang tapped the file folder on his desk. "It'll look good on your record."

"Or my résumé," Flint grumbled. "I have to be honest, sir. I don't like taking advantage of Maggie."

"Who says you will be? She must be as against

poachers as we are. She couldn't run that wild animal rehab if she wasn't."

"I wish I knew how she got involved with the Dodd Sanctuary. The first I'd heard of it was a few weeks ago."

"It's been keeping a low profile," Lang told him. "I get the idea that's partly your Maggie's idea, since she's running it by herself."

"And it's funded how?" Flint's green eyes narrowed. He didn't want to think of Maggie involved in anything shady, but a lot of time had passed since he last saw her. People could change.

"Abigail Dodd has more money than sense," Lang said, "and no children. She wants to leave a legacy, so she set up the sanctuary on the old Dodd Farm and hired Ms. Morgan because she knew her." He chuckled. "Believe you me, Abigail's close relatives are not pleased. I hear they tried to get her declared incompetent."

"And failed?"

"Big-time. By the time Maggie got done testifying, there was no way anybody could question the old lady's sanity."

"Maggie always did love the underdog and defended against injustices." Maybe that would make it easier to get her to talk to him. It was his job as a game warden to police the forest and wildlands, making sure no laws were broken and nature was preserved in its natural state.

Anybody who was hunting out of season was clearly being unfair, both to other hunters and to the animals.

Sighing in acceptance, he nodded. "Okay. Give me the file on the poaching so I can check for patterns. Is that their only crime?"

Lang handed him a manila folder. "Not by a long shot."

The colloquial reference to aiming from a distance did not sit well with Flint. Not well at all.

Wind whipped Maggie Morgan's long, honey-brown hair across her face as gathering clouds darkened the afternoon. Hurrying, she almost tripped over her enormous dog. "Out of the way, Wolfie. Mama has to finish her chores before the storm gets here."

If the black-and-brown canine hadn't bristled and begun to bark, she might not have noticed a familiar pickup truck heading up the long driveway to the sanctuary.

"Oh, hush, dog. You know the game warden. He was here just last week."

With a friendly wave to her approaching visitor, she went back to hauling armloads of fresh straw bedding. Whatever the guy wanted could wait until she'd tended to her patients' needs. Helpless animals always came first.

Approaching footsteps crinkled dry leaves behind her while Maggie was bent over spreading loose straw in a lean-to. She glanced through the bottom of the wire fence and saw black boots. "I'm almost done. How come you're back so soon? Did you bring me another patient?"

The Game and Fish warden cleared his throat. "Hello, Maggie."

That voice! Momentarily stunned, she froze. A shiver tickled her spine. It *couldn't* be him. Yet she knew it was.

The injured doe in the pen with her sensed her sudden nervousness and bolted, running across the enclosure and careening off the fencing.

"Easy, girl, easy." Maggie straightened and inched her way to the gate, slipping through and fastening it securely while steeling herself to turn and face her visitor. "Flint Crawford."

"You remember me."

How could she forget the man who had broken her heart and nearly ruined her life? She stalled by taking a moment to brush off her jeans and the sleeves of her denim jacket before she said, "Vaguely. What are you doing here?"

He spread his arms to display his dark green uniform and badge on an athletic body. "I work in Fulton County now. See?"

"I thought you were in the marines."

Flint nodded. "Long story. I missed home. Deep roots, I guess."

I don't believe a word of it. Maggie gritted her teeth rather than chance speaking. *If you had deep roots you'd have stayed here in the first place.*

Scattered drops the size of dimes were beginning to dot the dry ground. She extended her hands, palms up. "It's starting to rain."

"Can we take cover on the porch?"

"Why?"

"Talk, maybe?"

"I have nothing to say to you." The longer he lingered, the angrier Maggie grew. At this point she wasn't positive she could maintain her facade of calm indifference long enough for him to leave. Being in Flint's presence again was far more difficult than she'd imagined. Where were all the irate speeches she'd rehearsed for the past six years?

Silent, Maggie accompanied him toward his truck, the big dog at her heels. They began to circle the silver-gray pickup. Wolfie stiffened just as a deafening boom of thunder joined a blinding flash!

Everything blurred as Maggie was smacked hard on the shoulder, knocked off her feet and ended up lying in the dirt with Flint hovering over her. Wolfie was growling as he circled them.

She gave Flint a push. "Get off me!"

Instead, he supported himself on one arm and continued to keep her down. That was when she saw he'd drawn his gun. "No! Don't shoot my dog!"

"Hush," Flint ordered, getting to his knees. "Keep your head down."

"What are you babbling about? We almost got hit by lightning." The expression on his face argued otherwise. "Didn't we?"

"No. Thunder doesn't have a high-pitched echo. Whoever aimed at us expected the storm to mask a rifle shot."

Maggie tensed, blinking rapidly to try to clear her head. He was right! There had been a singing reverberation amid the rumbling noise of the storm.

She reached out for Wolfie, understanding a moment too late that that was a mistake.

The dog bared his fangs, lunged, and latched on to Flint's pant leg. Maggie screamed. Flint fell back, rolling farther behind the truck as he fought to break free.

Maggie barely registered the crack and whine of a second shot. A side window of the truck shattered. She screamed again and covered her head as glass rained down. Wolfie released his captive and made a beeline for her.

The game warden recovered enough to sit, pulled out a cell phone and called for assistance before turning to Maggie. "Help is on its way."

"Are you hurt? Did he bite through the skin?"

"Don't worry about me. How are you?"

"Fine."

"You don't look fine."

"I'm not used to being a target. Now I know how these poor wild animals must feel."

As Flint slowly reached toward her, she told herself to move away. Her knees felt welded to the ground.

His warm, strong hand cupped her cheek as scattered drops of rain continued to fall. A thumb brushed away blood. It took her a moment to realize it was hers. She jerked back and patted her face.

"You're not shot," Flint said. "I think a sliver of glass may have nicked you."

"Terrific."

She sat back on her heels. Flint's green gaze seemed almost tender. That fit. She'd always viewed him as a caring person, which was why his abandonment had shaken her so badly. Above all, she reasoned, she must keep reminding herself of his desertion.

"We're about to get soaked," she said flatly.

"Better wet than dead." Flint was rubbing his lower leg. "I hope the shooter gave up and left. Thanks to your dog I couldn't catch a hibernating turtle right now."

"Serves you right." A shiver skittered up her spine. "Do you think we're still in danger? I figure they're long gone."

"You're probably right. They've had plenty of time to sneak up on us and finish the job if they wanted to."

"Oh, that's comforting."

"I'm not trying to be comforting," Flint snapped back. "I'm trying to keep you alive."

Survival. He was right about that. She patted her pockets. She'd forgotten to bring her cell phone. "How long before we have that help you promised?"

"I don't know. We're pretty far out in the country."

"Then hand me your phone," Maggie said. "I need to make a call and I left mine inside." If it had been anyone but Flint, she would have added *please.*

She saw him hesitate.

"Okay, but keep it short. This is for official use only."

"Would you rather I made a run for the house to get my own?"

"No. Here."

Grabbing the phone before he changed his mind, she had to think hard to remember the number that was programmed into her own cell phone.

A tentative "Hello" was all the greeting she allowed before blurting, "Mom?"

"Maggie? I almost didn't answer. This isn't your number."

"No. I'm using a borrowed phone."

"What happened to yours?

"Never mind that. Please, just listen. I need

you to pick up Mark from school and keep him at your place until you hear from me. I'll explain everything later."

"But—"

"Please, Mom? This is really important."

"Okay, honey. But I'll expect all the details when you come get him. And plan to stay for supper. Bye!"

Sure, assuming I'm able to get rid of my unwelcome visitor by then. Maggie's fondest hope was that the shooter was attempting to scare the new game warden just on general principle. Given that this particular warden was Flint Crawford, she owed their anonymous assailant a debt of gratitude for trying.

Too bad it hadn't worked.

Police and sheriff's units arrived just ahead of an ambulance. Dressed for the heavier rain that was predicted, Sheriff Harlan Allgood leaned against the fender of the silver-gray Game and Fish truck and shook his head at Flint. "Sorry about this, son. Want me to help you over onto the porch where the medics are working on Maggie?"

"I won't be welcome. I can hop in the ambulance if this drizzle gets much worse."

"Suit yourself." He chuckled. "I didn't dream you'd run into trouble so soon. Who'd you manage to rile in a day and a half?"

"Beats me." Flint pulled the leg of his pants up to his knee. "Everybody's been pretty friendly so far." He grimaced. "Except for Maggie and her dog."

"Wolfie's always been fine around me," Harlan said. "What'd you do to set him off?"

"He was probably reacting to my knocking her down to keep her from getting shot."

"I reckon she gave you what for."

"Oh, yeah. She actually thought I was going to shoot her dog." Flint peered into the woods. "Any of your people come up with the real shooter yet?"

"Nope, and I don't expect 'em to. The ol' boys around these parts are good at disappearin'."

"Is this the first trouble Maggie's had?"

"Why don't you ask her?"

"Yeah, well, she and I aren't exactly on the best of terms."

"And that *surprises* you?" Harlan guffawed. "Folks around here still remember when you turned tail and skedaddled."

Flint refused to let the old-timer goad him. The details of the past were nobody's business but his and Maggie's. And speaking of the past, if he hadn't heard that both her brothers had left to establish successful careers in neighboring states, he might have blamed one of *them*.

"So, what are you going to do?" Flint asked.

"'Bout what?"

"Finding the shooter, to start with. And then protecting Maggie, just in case she's a target, too."

"Don't know what any of us can do," Harlan replied with a drawl. "I suppose I can have a deputy cruise by a time or two."

"Well, somebody'd better keep a lookout. We could have been killed."

Chuckling, the portly older man stepped away to give the medics room to check Flint's dog bite. "I doubt that. There ain't many hunters round here who'd miss unless they meant to. You ask me, those shots were a warning."

Flint grimaced as a paramedic disinfected his shin and slapped a small bandage on it. Harlan was right. Country boys grew up learning to hit what they were aiming at. Whoever was behind this attack had missed on purpose. If Maggie hadn't been standing next to him at the time of the shooting, *she* would have been his chief suspect.

As if his thoughts had drawn her, she spoke from behind them. "Do you need to see proof of Wolfie's vaccinations, Sheriff?"

Harlan shook his head. "Not unless Flint here wants to check 'em."

"I trust you," Flint said. "I'm just surprised you let that dog wander loose where he can bite people."

Maggie huffed. "I don't suppose you'd believe

he's hardly ever growled at anybody else in the four years since I rescued him."

"Honestly?"

"Scout's honor," she replied. "He usually barks to tell me someone's here, but that's about all."

Flint swallowed hard. Maybe he should have stayed in Serenity almost six years ago, for Maggie's sake, but when she'd refused to even consider eloping he'd decided she didn't truly love him. In retrospect, he'd wondered if she'd simply been defying her parents by dating him in the first place.

As the years had passed, he'd been forced to admit that their teenage romance had been doomed. Perhaps they'd been overly attracted to each other because the relationship was forbidden by both their feuding families. It was certainly a possibility.

And now? Flint studied her closed expression. He and Maggie were very different people. Besides, plenty of gossip had made its way to him since his recent return, and her phone call to her mom had confirmed it. Maggie was a single mother. Clearly, she had moved on and he'd better do the same. Too bad he'd been assigned to renew their acquaintance.

What puzzled Flint was how Captain Lang had learned about their ill-fated romance. Stories about it could have come up when the department had been researching Elwood Witherspoon and his kin, he supposed. There was no way to discuss Witherspoon and his relatives without mentioning their long-standing feud with the Crawfords. And the way Flint had chosen distance as a means of defusing the mounting tension would certainly have come up.

Maggie's deep-seated anger surprised him, though, particularly since he had yet to broach the subject of her uncle's whereabouts. Hadn't she read any of his letters? Didn't she understand he'd acted in the best interests of them both? Even if she disagreed with his choices, surely she could see things from his perspective.

Flint pushed those thoughts aside. Until the police figured out who had taken a potshot at them, they'd both have to be on guard. He had combat training. Maggie did not. Therefore, since the sheriff wouldn't take special precautions to protect her, he would have to look into the cause and come up with some answers. Whether she liked it or not. And stay alive in the process.

And speaking of things she was not going to like, he figured he might as well get it over with so he said, "By the way, can you tell me where your uncle Elwood is living these days?"

"What does he have to do with this?"

"Probably nothing. I just need to locate him and have a little talk."

She rolled her eyes. "I have no idea where he is, nor do I care."

This was not going to be easy at all.

TWO

Maggie phoned her mother again to make sure Mark was safe, then fidgeted until Flint and the police finally finished their rainy investigating and drove away. If the sun had not set, she wondered if they'd have prowled around even longer.

Combing her long hair more to one side to cover the tiny butterfly bandage on her cheek, she grabbed her purse and headed for her truck. Wolfie leaped in before she finished saying, "Yes, you can go."

Smiling, Maggie slid behind the wheel and started for town, noting how her fingers didn't want to hold still. She wasn't wired because of seeing Flint. *No, sir.* Being shot at was the problem. It had made her "jumpy as a baby chick at a possum party," as her daddy used to say.

Harlan hadn't mentioned any names, but she knew who he probably blamed for the shooting. It hurt to think that the most likely suspect was her own great-uncle, but there was no getting around it. Elwood Witherspoon was a throwback to the days when country people had settled their own quarrels. A lot of old-timers still talked a good fight, but they weren't serious. Elwood was. He delighted in using history as an excuse to break current laws. Worse, he was teaching his three grandsons to follow in his footsteps.

Maggie grasped the wheel tighter. Even a mean-looking dog was no protection against an enemy with a rifle, kin or not. And if the target happened to be wearing the forest green uniform and badge of a game warden in Elwood's neck of the woods, he might as well have a bull's-eye painted on his back.

Since the shooting, she had begun to feel as vulnerable as she had after her testimony at Abigail's competency hearing. The old woman's niece and nephew, Missy and Sonny Dodd, had threatened to shut down the sanctuary as soon as they got the chance, and had blamed Maggie for their loss in court.

Now somebody else was threatening her and Flint was involved this time. In a rural place like Serenity, danger could lurk in every shadow, behind every tree. Her agitated state caused her to picture new threats at each twist and turn of the nearly deserted road.

Already wired, Maggie overreacted when headlights gleamed behind her, blinding her with their glare. She accelerated. It didn't help. The vehicle kept closing the distance between them.

Maggie's heart began pounding so hard she could count the beats at her temples. Every muscle was taut. The nearer the follower drew, the higher his headlights appeared. It had to be a truck—a lot bigger than hers.

A highway passing lane was coming up. Suppose the other driver's actions were nothing more than a result of her slower speed and overactive imagination? Maybe if she hit her brakes...

She whispered, "Please, God?" and lightly tapped the brake pedal to flash her stoplights.

The larger truck slammed into her rear bumper and sent Wolfie flying at the dash despite her outthrust arm. Dazed and shaking his huge head, he climbed back onto the seat beside her and licked her cheek.

"Oh, baby, I'm sorry."

Normally she'd pull over and see if there had been any damage to her vehicle, but not this time. Not here where there were no houses or lights. And certainly not after what had happened earlier, at home. She swung into the far right lane as soon as the road divided for easy passing.

"No, no, no!" The lights were coming at her again! Faster than before. She held tight to the wheel with her left hand and grabbed Wolfie's collar with her right. "Lord, help us!"

As if in answer to the frantic prayer, the headlights swung to her left. Had her panic been for nothing? What a foolish mistake.

Releasing the dog, Maggie put both hands back on the steering wheel. As the other vehicle drew even, she glanced over at it, expecting to see young men, waving beer cans and whooping it up.

There was only the driver. What a surprise. She could tell he'd turned his head to look at her, but it was too dark to make out his features.

"As soon as he passes I'll get his license plate number so I can report reckless driving," she told herself, reaching into her purse to feel around for a pen.

In that split second of inattention the other driver swerved. The trucks collided. Metal scraped, bent, squealed.

Maggie fought to stay on the pavement. An inch more to the right and her tires would slip onto the muddy shoulder!

The truck shimmied. Wolfie barked. Maggie did her best to maintain control. It was no use. She hollered, "Hang on, boy," as the outside wheels edged a fraction too far and carried them off the road with a lurch.

They bent a mile marker post, then bumped and jostled down the rain-slick grass slope and slid diagonally toward a barbed-wire fence at the bottom.

If Maggie tried to steer while sideways on the

steep incline, she knew, she would lose control and roll. All she could do was ride it out. And pray.

Flint was finishing an enjoyable evening meal at the Allgood residence and discussing who might have been behind the shooting at the animal rehab center when the sheriff's phone rang.

Harlan answered and listened briefly. "Well, what're you callin' me for?" Flint saw him begin to scowl. "Okay, okay. I'll head out there ASAP. Where'd you say it was?"

Flint pushed back from the table. "What's happened?"

"Single-car accident. A truck skidded off Highway 62 out by the Anderson place."

"Anybody hurt?"

"The witness didn't know."

"Why are you responding? Can't the highway patrol handle it?"

The sheriff nodded as he buckled his utility belt and checked his gun. "Probably. They've been called, too." He tilted his head at Flint. "You might wanna grab your gear and come along."

"Why? Was a deer involved?" That kind of collision occurred often during the fall of the year.

"Don't know. Don't think so."

Puzzled, Flint pulled his jacket on over his

bulletproof vest. "Okay. If you think you need me, I'll come with you."

"It ain't for my sake," Harlan said as he kissed his wife's cheek and hurried to the kitchen door. "It's for yours. The witness says the truck's from Maggie's job. Nobody drives it but her."

The vehicle that had slammed into Maggie had kept going. As soon as her truck stopped sliding, she turned off the ignition key and unbuckled her seat belt. She and Wolfie were okay. That was the important thing.

Taking a moment to collect herself, she buried her face in her pet's ruff and silently thanked God, then sat back. "Well, what do you think, Wolfie? Shall we hike up to the road and flag somebody down?"

As Maggie's random thoughts began to sort themselves out, she realized she had a better way to summon help. She reached for her phone. Her purse wasn't on the seat anymore. Feeling around on the floor of the cab didn't help, either.

She tried to shoulder open her door. It was stuck. Thankfully, the passenger side worked. Wolfie cleared her with a bound and began leaping through long, wet grasses and wildflowers like a spring lamb at play.

"Stay with me, boy, while I find my phone."

Ignoring her, he began to sniff at their surroundings while she stood in the thigh-high grass to explore beneath the seat. Her fingers touched soft leather. Got it! However, as she pulled her purse out she noted that it felt far too light. Half its contents were missing.

"Rats!" She leaned in and patted along the floor mat. The cell phone had to be there. Too bad she didn't have a flashlight.

Wolfie's sharp yelp made her jerk. The barrage of angry barking that followed was unmistakable. He was defending her. But from what?

Maggie had held very still when he began to bark. Now she slowly backed out of the truck cab and scanned their surroundings.

Hackles up, her dog was looking past her toward the road. A vehicle was idling on the shoulder of the highway and someone was getting out. She cupped a hand around her mouth and shouted, "Have you called 911?"

The dark figure merely stood there. Wouldn't an innocent passerby answer? Ask if she was injured?

"Hello? Do you have a phone?"

Flustered, she peered up at the other truck. Not only was it the same size and color as the one that had hit her, but the part of it that she could see looked uneven!

Maggie reached across and clicked off her headlights. Suppose that was no Good Samaritan up there? Suppose it was her unknown enemy? Had he come back to finish the job he'd started?

Frightened, Maggie gave up the search for her missing phone and edged around the front of her truck. Wolfie was already on the opposite side of the barbed-wire fence separating the roadway from a pasture. Climbing back up to the pavement to flag down a passing motorist was out of the question at this point. So, what options were left?

She could stand there until her nemesis decided to make the next move, or she could take matters into her own hands. Undecided, she studied him. She had Wolfie on her side and the other driver had...a gun! The glint of a chromed pistol in his hand was brief but quite enough incentive.

Maggie whirled and raced to the section of fence her dog had shimmied under, dropped onto her stomach and crawled through the way a commando would.

A gruff shout echoed. "You can't hide."

That actually helped. She rose to all fours, sprang to her feet and ran, positive she heard someone in pursuit. Wolfie paced her for a few moments before diverting toward the nearest patch of woods.

"Good boy." Maggie followed, panting. At least one of them was thinking straight.

Forest shadows swallowed her. She slipped on wet leaves beneath the trees, falling and recovering over and over until her energy and adrenaline were spent.

Hands resting on the muddy knees of her jeans, she gasped for breath. Wolfie circled back and licked her face.

Prayer was called for, she knew, but her heart was too dispirited to even try.

Kneeling in the wet leaves she slipped an arm around her dog's neck and let tears be her unspoken plea.

Nobody knew where she was but God.

And her enemy.

Flint used his emergency flashers and made better time than the sheriff. Spying a cluster of headlights along the opposite shoulder, he knew this was the accident scene. Maggie had almost made it into town. Why in the world had she run off the road? Was she speeding? Talking or texting? Had she lost focus for some other reason?

None of those ideas made sense. The teenage Maggie he remembered had been conscientious to a fault. Surely her basic nature hadn't changed that much.

Flint parked in an open spot on his side of the highway so he wouldn't have to make a U-turn and left his hazard lights on as a warning to passing drivers.

Traffic was sparse. He jogged across all four lanes in seconds. Several civilian motorists had stopped and were pointing to the wreck. A uniformed police officer at the base of the incline cupped a hand around his mouth and shouted, "No sign of the driver."

Flint's heart beat hard and fast. If Maggie wasn't there, where was she? Had she been kidnapped? No. That idea was too far-fetched. But why leave her truck? Nothing made sense.

He stepped off the outer berm, slipping and sliding his way to the bottom. Plenty of others had obviously been down there, because the vegetation was trampled. What if their carelessness had destroyed evidence that would lead to finding her?

Pulling the flashlight off his utility belt, he played the beam over the scene.

Someone touched his arm. "Simmer down," a deputy said. "As soon as the sheriff gets organized, we'll form a search party. We'll find her."

"What about her dog? Has anybody seen a big dog that looks like a wolf? They're usually together."

The officer radioed to the top of the embankment, "Any of you guys see Maggie's dog?"

Flint felt like a fool. They all knew her and Wolfie and probably cared more than he did. She was one of their own. So why was the urge to track her down so strong in him?

He walked away, playing his light over the ground as he went. Except for the trampled area around the truck, there was no sign of her. Still, he refused to give up. The minute a search party formed, he'd join it, whether anybody liked it or not. He was going to help hunt for her, period. He was...

The beam of his light reflected off drops of rain clinging to the barbed wire. The whole fence glistened, except for one narrow place on the bottom strand! Flint's breath caught. If nobody else had knocked off the water, there was a chance that Maggie and her dog had done so in passing. Hopefully, they were the only two.

He waved his light like a beacon and shouted, "Over here! I think she went through here."

Nobody paid attention. He tried again. A few bystanders waved back and continued to talk among themselves, but other than that, he was ignored. Delaying only long enough to shout at the closest officer, "Tell Sheriff Allgood that I think the victim went through the pasture fence just south of here," Flint went into action.

Once he got through the fence, it was harder to tell which way Maggie and Wolfie had gone. The pasture was already springing back. That slowed his progress. Bent grass, broken stems and an occasional crushed weed were all he had to go by.

The faint path turned so abruptly Flint almost missed the clues. It looked as though Maggie was headed for the woods where her passing would leave no crushed grass.

That should make it harder for him to track

her. Fortunately, it would do the same for whoever she was fleeing from—unless there was more than one person after her and they could fan out to cover a wider area.

Picking up his pace, Flint prayed he'd reach Maggie before anyone else did. Before it was too late.

THREE

Being born and raised in the country gave Maggie an advantage. Not knowing exactly where she was took much of it away. Most Ozark homes and farms weren't located too far apart, but there were also untouched acres of forest that had claimed canyons, and any other land too rocky for pasture or crops.

Spent and discouraged, Maggie sat on a protruding shelf of shale while she caught her breath. Moonlight came and went as wind from the earlier storm pushed lingering clouds across the sky. Sheet lightning flashed in the distance, providing a snapshot view of her surroundings.

She closed her eyes and folded her hands to pray, but only chaotic thoughts resulted. They darted madly through her mind like tiny fish in the shallows when a shadow fell over the water. Thoughts of *rescue* kept recurring. So did *divine guidance*. And—*Flint?*

Maggie's eyes popped open. "No. Not Flint.

Anybody but him." Surely God could send someone else to save her.

The soft sound of her voice drew the weary dog and she draped an arm across his shoulders the way she would have a human friend. "Yes, Wolfie, I have you, don't I? And if I was sure you wouldn't stop to chase rabbits all the way home, I'd let you lead me."

She sighed. "We couldn't stay with the truck. But I kind of wish I'd aimed for the lights of farmhouses along the highway instead of following you into the wilderness."

He slurped her cheek and ear.

"Yeah, well, maybe your path was best, but now what?"

The dog stiffened as if in reply. His nose twitched and he lifted it to face the breeze, then raised his hackles.

Maggie tensed. Listened. Held her breath until her body forced her to exhale. What she had thought was the sound of her panting dog was actually farther away, in the direction she believed they had come. It wasn't loud. And it faded from time to time, but it was definitely there.

She stood slowly, dismayed by a wave of dizziness. Pushing herself to the edge of her endurance was one thing, but this consequence was unexpected. How could she run when she could hardly keep her balance? And what if she fainted?

"I have never fainted in my life and I'm not going to start now," Maggie insisted in a whisper. Wolfie wagged his bushy tail.

Demanding that her body comply, she turned to start up the slope behind them. The third step dropped her against the trunk of an enormous oak and there she stayed while bright flashes of color danced at the edges of her vision and the forest seemed to vibrate. This was not good.

Beside her, Wolfie began to growl.

Maggie followed his line of sight, seeing nothing but drifting, shimmering, moonlit shadows. Clearly, she was not going any farther, so what could she use as a defensive weapon?

A nearby deadfall caught her eye. She managed to break a portion of a loose, rotting limb from the fallen tree. It wasn't much of a club, but at least it wasn't too heavy to wield. She'd played baseball as a child. It was time for a little batting practice. Even if she only got one swing, it was better than just standing there.

"Wolfie, heel," Maggie ordered quietly. "Down. Stay."

Resting the section of limb on her shoulder, she propped herself behind the massive oak and waited.

A twig snapped. Wolfie started to rise, but the flat of Maggie's hand in front of his nose stopped him. It wouldn't be long now. Truth to tell, she was looking forward to clocking the guy who had run her off the road.

She tensed. The dog was quivering beside her, as ready as she was. Another cracking sound. Heavy breathing. Almost there!

Fight-or-flight emotions gave her a needed jolt of energy. She poised and mustered her strength, waiting for just the right moment to swing.

Tracking had been part of Flint's job training. He'd temporarily lost Maggie's trail when she crossed a field of exposed rock, but he knew she couldn't be far ahead.

Should he call to her? No. That might tip off anyone who was stalking her. He couldn't chance it.

Bending low to inspect a patch of disturbed leaves, he sensed imminent danger and began to rise.

Flint's forearm came up just in time to absorb most of the blow. Bits of rotted wood rained down like snowflakes. He shouted, "Officer of the law" as he ducked to the side to avoid further strikes and drew his sidearm.

His flashlight found its target. Someone was preparing to hit him again. "Freeze!"

In a heartbeat, he understood. Maggie had thought he was her enemy and had defended herself. Bravo for her. Too bad her aim was so good.

He raised both hands, diverting the light and the gun. "It's me. Maggie, it's me. You're safe now."

Flint holstered his pistol while she processed reality. He flicked off the flashlight in case there was danger nearby and ruffled his hair to brush away bits of wood.

"Drop the limb, Maggie," he said, keeping his voice low. "You're safe now. You're safe."

Slowly, her arms lowered. The fractured branch fell. She began to blink rapidly and her balance wavered. Flint reached out to catch her and she fell into his arms, clinging as if he were the only lifeline in a sea of hungry sharks.

What could he do? He tightened his embrace, held her close and waited for her to relax. Eternity passed. Flint was so overcome with emotional memory he squeezed his eyes shut and prayed for strength. This hurt. Deeply. It was as if no time had passed; as if he and Maggie were once again in love and looking forward to a bright future together.

Reality saved him when Wolfie whined. Maggie pushed him away. The look in her eyes was unreadable. His conscience insisted he apologize. "I'm sorry. I thought you were going to faint."

"I never…" She began to nod. "Thanks. I am woozy. I guess I ran too far and too fast."

Flint held up a hand. "Hold on a second and you can tell me everything." He pulled out his phone and reported that she was safe, then led her to the nearest rock outcropping so she could rest and recover, trusting the dog to alert if anyone else approached.

"Okay. What happened?"

"A big truck ran me off the road."

"I could tell that something did. Why did you run?"

"Because he came back!" Her voice faltered. "I—I thought he was going to finish me."

"Why? Who has it in for you?"

Her shoulders sagged. "Nobody. At least not lately."

"Explain."

"Do you remember Abigail Dodd? She used to teach in the old rock school. My mother was one of her students."

"What about her?"

"She's the one who thought of starting the wildlife rescue here. I had just graduated from school to become a veterinary assistant, and when she couldn't find a real vet to take the management job, she offered it to me."

"Why would that make anybody shoot at you and run you off the road?"

Maggie huffed. "I testified on Abigail's behalf. Her nephew actually threatened me after the competency hearing and her niece glared daggers. I wouldn't put it past either of them to shoot at me. What I don't understand is why they waited until now."

"The sheriff mentioned something about that hearing, but he never told me you'd been threatened. He just said Ms. Dodd's relatives were unhappy about the verdict."

"That's an understatement. Missy and Sonny were fit to be tied. They wanted power of attorney. I'm the reason they didn't get it."

Flint listened with concern. "Do you think it was one of them who ran you off the road tonight?"

"I can't think of anybody else who's that mad at me. Maybe they figure they'll have a better shot at their aunt's money if I don't stand in their way."

"You do realize how paranoid that sounds, don't you?"

"It's only paranoia if nobody is really out to get me. After two tries, including tonight, I wonder."

By the time the sheriff's men arrived on ATVs to take Flint and her back to the road, Maggie had regained most of her strength. The official pronouncement that her truck was still safe to drive helped even more.

"I'm fine," she insisted to a crowd of men. "I can get to my mother's by myself."

Harlan seemed reluctant to allow it. Flint looked angry.

She faced them, hands on her hips. "You agree

my wheels are safe and it's only a couple more miles to town. What's your problem?"

"You are," Flint argued. "An hour ago you were hardly able to stand. What makes you think you're capable of driving?"

"An hour ago I was scared to death," she countered. "Now that nobody's chasing me, I'm fine."

"What about later?"

"I'll worry about tomorrow, tomorrow," Maggie said. "Consider the lilies of the field—"

"Don't quote scripture to me."

"You *know* that verse?"

"I know a lot of Bible verses."

"Since when?"

"Since I almost got my head blown off in combat," Flint said.

Maggie sobered. "Was that the real reason you left the marines?" She could tell by the set of his jaw and shoulders that she'd hit a nerve, but his answer was ambiguous.

"I stayed until my enlistment was up," Flint said. "Stop trying to change the subject. You're in no shape to drive that truck and you know it."

"On the contrary. I'm perfectly capable of taking care of myself. I thought I proved that when I clobbered you back in the woods."

"All you proved was that you're no match for a gun."

"Nonsense." Maggie was not about to admit she'd been weak and ineffectual when she faced what she'd believed was her enemy. "If I hadn't recognized you, I'd have hit you again."

"With a limb so rotten it fell apart?"

It had to be pulpy in order to be light enough for her to lift, Maggie thought with chagrin. "I wasn't helpless. I could have grabbed a rock after you went down. I was tired, that's all." She turned to the sheriff. "What about the truck that hit me? Have you found any clues?"

Harlan shook his head. "Not to speak of. There's a bit of dark paint on your fender, but that's about all. We took a scraping in case we end up having to send something to the crime lab in Little Rock."

"Meaning, if whoever ran me off the road doesn't bother me again nothing will be done?" Maggie folded her arms across her chest to hide a shiver.

"We'll see. I wouldn't worry much. Accidents happen. There's usually nothing sinister about them."

Beside her, Flint raised his voice. "I don't believe you people. Did you know she was threatened by Ms. Dodd's relatives?"

"Ah, Sonny was just blowin' off steam. Now calm down." The sheriff gave him a tight smile. "You've been away too long. You know this ain't a big city. We don't have serious trouble around here. Leastwise not much."

No serious trouble? Maggie recalled tales of

the days when clannishness had divided the town better than any city gang wars could have. Much of what she'd heard as a child had probably been embellished, of course. Small-town gossip was famous for that. Still, it wouldn't hurt to look into that, too. Now that Flint was home, there was an outside chance her elderly uncle might be involved for reasons other than his poaching. He was hardheaded enough to want to nurture his hatred of the Crawfords and rekindle the generations-old family feud.

What caused her additional worry was the fact that she seemed to be a target, too, probably thanks to her need to tolerate Flint's presence for the sake of her job. It had been easy to blame rancor against Flint for the shots at the animal center. This so-called accident put a totally different spin on things. This wasn't a bullet, but it was aimed at her. Was this truly an accident, as the sheriff assumed, or were the incidents related?

Leaving Harlan and Flint arguing, Maggie circled her truck with Wolfie and climbed in. She didn't have to look in her mirrors to know what she'd see. Flint was going to look fit to be tied.

A lopsided smile lifted her lips—and her spirits. He'd looked so relieved when he found her in the woods she almost hated to annoy him. But she had her limits. Life had forced her to stand on her own two feet, and she wasn't about to let the man who had almost ruined her life take it over. Not now. Not ever. She had been doing fine by herself, raising her son and providing for him with little outside help from anyone except her mother.

Maggie's heart warmed at the thought of Mark and Mom. They had been so good for each other: Mark comforting Faye after she was widowed and Faye becoming the grandmother the boy needed to balance his life. It was the perfect arrangement for them all. One she intended to preserve.

As Maggie saw it, all she had to do was pinpoint who was so upset with her—or mad because she'd been seen with Flint—and was acting out. Country people might be obstinate at times, but they were logical thinkers. Sensible and honorable. With God's help she'd figure out who'd been stirring up trouble.

Her hands tightened on the steering wheel. She hoped nothing altered the peaceful life she'd made for herself in Serenity. If she truly trusted the Lord in everything, she'd be fine. However, the line between self-confidence and letting go and allowing her heavenly Father to guide her could be blurry, especially if she intended to assert her will, which she did.

"Okay, okay," Maggie said, frustrated. She cast her eyes to the heavens momentarily. "I'll try to understand and do things Your way, Father, but I'm sure bumfuzzled right now."

Flint stood with the sheriff and watched Maggie pull away. He shook his head. "That woman is the most stubborn, impossible person I have ever met."

"Yup. That's what keeps her going," Harlan replied with a grin. "She's quite mule-headed, our Maggie."

"She never used to be."

"Times change. Kids grow up. She was only sixteen when you left, right?"

"Almost seventeen. I was eighteen."

"And you were skinny as a rail, if I remember right. No wonder you hit the road."

"Beg pardon?"

Harlan snorted. "Her brothers mighta kilt you, son. Both of 'em outweighed ya by a bunch, and they sure didn't want you dating their sister."

"You're telling me." Flint sighed. "I tried to get her to elope, you know. She wouldn't hear of it. Faye had always said she wanted to put on a big wedding for her only daughter, and Maggie was determined to do things her mother's way."

"Probably for the best." The older man lit up a cigar and puffed it slowly. "Did you ever get hitched?"

"Nope. Not even close."

"Hmm. Maggie was engaged a couple of times

but never went through with those weddings. After her father passed away she was pretty much tied to her mother."

"I suppose that worked out for the best, since she needed Faye's help with the baby."

"You know about Mark?"

Flint shrugged. "I heard a little gossip last week."

"Hmm." The sheriff blew smoke rings. "Well, I'd best be going. You coming back to the house with me for dessert? My Wanda's baked one a' her prize-winnin' apple pies. Takes a blue ribbon at the fair every year."

"Back to town? Sure," Flint answered quickly.

That made Harlan chuckle. "I thought I'd swing by Faye's on the way, just to make sure Maggie got there safe. You might as well follow me."

Of course he would. And while they were relaxed and eating pie, he intended to quiz the sheriff a lot more. Harlan was obviously relying on good-old-boy mentality to figure things out when there was a good chance sinister forces were at work instead. Just because there hadn't been much crime in Serenity in the past didn't mean there wasn't any now.

Flint didn't care whether locals like the Dodds were involved or not. The important thing was putting an end to the threats before somebody got hurt. *Before Maggie got hurt.*

Her unseen enemies had already gotten too close for comfort. They had to be positively identified and stopped. And if the sheriff wasn't going to follow through, somebody had to take up the cause.

Flint's badge and gun made him a full-fledged law officer.

He intended to act like one.

FOUR

It didn't bother Maggie one bit to note that Sheriff Allgood had caught up and was following her. As they drove into town and streetlights glinted off the light bar atop his patrol car, she realized that he wasn't the only one. The third vehicle in line looked suspiciously like an official Game and Fish truck.

Maggie whipped into her mother's driveway and waited, more than ready to face down Flint and send him on his way if he stopped. When both drivers cruised on past, however, she wasn't sure whether to be relieved or disappointed. Yes, she was glad for an armed escort. No, she was not happy that Flint had tagged along behind. Yes, she appreciated the sheriff's concern. And no, she...

Maggie chewed on her lower lip. What was wrong with her? She hadn't felt normal since her first glimpse of Warden Crawford, and things were getting more complicated by the minute.

Faye threw open her front door, flooding the yard with light. "Maggie? Arc you all right?"

"Finc, Mom. Shut the door. I'll be right in."

When her mother didn't listen, Maggie shouted, "I said, shut the door."

Faye stood, silhouetted in the backlight as if making herself an intentional target. Worse, Mark had joined her. The maternal instinct in Maggie spurred her to make a dash for the porch, scoop up her son and rush everyone back inside. The last thing to pass through before the door slammed was Wolfie's tail.

"What in the world is going on?" Faye asked.

"Sorry I yelled at you."

"Never mind that. Why is your face as pale as my legs after a long winter?"

Despite her mother's attempt at humor, Maggie knew she sensed trouble. "It's complicated." Putting Mark down, she kissed his cheek before saying, "Why don't you take Wolfie and go play, honey?"

"Mamaw said I could have ice cream when you came."

"After supper. Now go. Wolfie gets bored when you're at school. He misses you."

"I miss him, too." With that, the child took off, his furry friend trotting along beside him.

"Let's go in the kitchen while I reheat the food

and you can tell me all about what's been going on," Faye said.

Nodding, Maggie followed, plopping into her favorite place at the table and raking trembling fingers through her hair. "It's a long story."

"We have time. I already fed Mark." She poured two cups of coffee and set one in front of her weary daughter. "Why don't you start with your first call to me this afternoon? Why did I need to pick up my grandson?"

"Because somebody was shooting near my place." Maggie wrapped her hands around the warm mug.

"Surely not at you!"

"I think the shots were meant to scare off the game warden."

"That's silly. Why would anybody bother a warden out there? They're always around."

"Not this guy," Maggie said, steeling her nerves for the predictable reaction when she added, "This warden was new. It was Flint Crawford."

Faye choked and sputtered. Maggie patted her back until she stopped coughing enough to ask, "Who?"

"You heard me. I didn't get a chance to ask him much, but he did say he's left the military and gone into law enforcement." She made a face. "Isn't that special?"

"What are we going to do?"

"Nothing, for the present. I actually thought the shooter might be Uncle Elwood when it first happened. You know how he hates wardens and Crawfords."

"What changed your mind?"

With a deep sigh, Maggie told her, "Somebody ran me off the road tonight."

Faye grabbed her arm. "Are you okay?"

"Yes."

"But what happened? Where? How?"

As Maggie began to cite details, she managed to omit Flint's part in her rescue. Anyone could have tracked her. He just happened to be handy, that's all.

And why was that? she asked herself. Of all the possibilities, why would God—or the sheriff—send the one man she desperately wanted to avoid? Moreover, why would Flint volunteer? There were lots of men who knew the area better than he did, particularly since he'd been away for six years.

High-pitched, childish laughter drifted from the living room. Mark was happy. Contented. Safe. Was that about to change?

Maggie rose and refilled both coffee mugs. "So, what are your thoughts? Do you think Elwood heard Flint was back and tracked him down at my place? Would he be angry enough to shoot around me when I might accidentally be hit?"

"I don't know. I'd hoped he'd mellowed in his old age."

"He was worse in the *past*?" She was astounded. "That's a surprise."

"It wouldn't be if you knew the whole story. It's what actually started the feud between my people, the Witherspoons, and the Crawford family."

"Go on."

Sighing, Faye complied. "I didn't see any of this firsthand, of course, but the story hasn't changed much since the beginning. Elwood, his dad and his brother were all drafted. Ira Crawford was—"

"Flint's *grandfather* Ira?"

"Actually, his great-grandfather. As the youngest, Ira was about the same age as Elwood even though they were technically a generation apart. People had big families in those days and sometimes aunts and uncles were as young as their own nieces and nephews. Anyway, Ira's leg had been damaged in a logging accident, so he wasn't called up like the other men were."

"They were jealous? That seems like a pretty lame reason for a feud—no pun intended."

"No, no. That wasn't the problem. The Witherspoons asked Ira to look after their farm, since the properties were adjoining and they'd been friends for years. They trusted him."

"Ooookay." Maggie could tell that her mother was struggling to present the tale accurately and having difficulty keeping her account unbiased. "I knew Elwood always had a chip on his shoulder. Was it because he didn't think Ira did a good enough job?"

"Oh, no. Ira did a great job. In more ways than one. Unfortunately, his choices benefited himself, not his former friends."

Losing patience, Maggie wanted to insist that her mom get to the core of the problems and had to struggle to keep from interrupting.

"Elwood was the only man in his immediate family to survive combat," Faye said sadly. "He never lost hope of returning to his waiting bride. She'd wanted to get married before he shipped out, but the family had resisted because she was so young."

Pausing, Faye sipped her coffee, then cleared her throat. "Here's where it gets complicated. While Elwood was gone, his best friend, Ira, took care of his farm by straightening some crooked fences and claiming a water source that generations of Witherspoons had counted on."

"That's terrible. No wonder Elwood was upset."

"Oh, it gets worse. The land wasn't the only thing Ira stole. He courted and married Elwood's intended. She became Bess Crawford, Flint's great-grandmother."

"Oh, my…" Maggie's hand covered her mouth. "Bess and Elwood? That seems awfully far-fetched."

"Now maybe. Not back then. Elwood was a handsome young man. But Ira had two advantages. He was injured, so he could play on her sympathies, and he was here, on the spot, while Elwood was overseas, perhaps dying in battle the way his kin had. By the time the dust settled, Ira was a prosperous farmer and rancher and Elwood had nothing left to come home to."

"But he did come back. He's still here."

"True. He eventually married, but it didn't last. His ex got custody of his only son. After that final loss he was never the same. That was when he became a recluse and moved away from civilization. In more ways than one." She was slowly shaking her head. "I can't say I blame him."

"What about the feud stories? Did the families really kill each other's shirttail relatives?"

"That's what they say."

"Then how come some survived?"

Faye shrugged. "Who knows? A lot can happen in sixty, seventy years. The law was stretched even thinner back then than it is now. They were never real keen on stirring up the old fight by asking too many questions, so unless somebody made a big stink, nothing was done."

"Unbelievable. I almost feel sorry for Elwood, even though I suspect he's been poaching."

"Do you have proof?" Faye asked, dishing up a plate of spaghetti and meatballs and placing it in front of Maggie.

"Thanks." She savored the spicy aroma for a moment before answering, "I thought I did. When somebody took a potshot at the warden today, I was just about positive."

"You could still be right," her mother remarked.

Maggie forked in a delectable mouthful and nodded. "I could. But it doesn't explain why I was forced off the road tonight."

"Probably just an accident."

"That's what the sheriff said." Maggie didn't believe that for a second. She stifled a shiver. Somebody had purposely tried to injure her— or worse—and until she figured out who, she'd have to be doubly vigilant.

Not to mention trying to keep Flint from seeing her son, she added, growing so uneasy she could barely force herself to continue eating. He was not going to be a happy camper once he realized whose child Mark must bc. When Mark was a baby she'd refused to admit anything. However, as time had passed, he'd grown to closely resemble his daddy.

No one but her mother had speculated aloud about Mark's origin, at least not in Maggie's presence. While Flint was away, it had been easier to keep her secret. Now that he was back in town, it was only a matter of time until disturbing rumors reached him.

Maggie knew she should stay ahead of the gossip and tell Flint everything. And she would. She must. The sooner the better.

She put down her fork and pushed her plate away. The butterflies in her stomach were keeping the delicious food from settling. As a lovelorn teenager, she'd found that convincing herself that Flint didn't care helped her cope. Then, as time had passed, she'd hardened her heart by assuming she'd never see him again.

So, what now? Explain? How? She huffed. Managing that was going to be impossible without making him furious, whether he was happy about being a father or hated the idea.

"Not hungry?" Faye asked.

"Too much on my mind."

"The shooting or the accident?"

Maggie shook her head. "Neither. Flint."

"That is a problem."

"Ya think?" Maggie rolled her eyes before glancing toward the living room where Mark and Wolfie were playing. "Any ideas about what I should do next?"

"Praying always helps me," Faye said as she cleared the table.

"Okay, what do I ask for? I used to pray Flint would come back to me, but he didn't."

"Really?"

Maggie noted her mother's raised eyebrows. "I meant when I needed him, not now."

"In whose opinion?"

"Oh, no. No way." She was shaking her head. "My life is in order and I'm happy. This is a *terrible* time for Flint to suddenly show up."

"Well, he did, and since you say he has a job here, I expect he's planning to stay. Maybe he's turned over a new leaf and is hoping you'll take him back."

"That's not why he transferred." Maggie pulled a face. "He told me it was because Bess and Ira needed help."

"Oh, dear. That certainly complicates things."

Maggie agreed. "I had no idea how much until you told me the whole feud story. Elwood may not even care that Flint's a game warden. He may hate him more because he's helping his great-grandparents. For all I know, Flint may be living with them on the farm the way he used to when he was a kid."

"Sounds like we should both pray for peace before we ask the Lord for anything else. I'll have a chat with Harlan the next time I see him, too."

That comment drew a slight smile from Maggie. "You mean you don't rely totally on prayers?"

Faye chuckled. "Prayers come first. But the way I see it, there's nothing wrong with depending on the people God has put in my life, as well. He gave us brains. I imagine He expects us to use them. And if that means alerting the sheriff, then that's what I'll do."

"You're going to tell him everything?"

"About the feud, yes. Any conclusions he chooses to draw regarding my grandson will be up to him. I don't suppose there are too many folks who don't already suspect who Mark's daddy is."

"That's what I'm afraid of."

"Well, don't be. You made a mistake, turned your life around and God forgave you. Besides, you ended up with a beautiful child. That can't be bad."

"Then why do I feel so guilty?" She began to pace. "If only Flint hadn't left when he did."

"What excuse did he give?" Faye asked.

"None. One day he was here and the next he was gone. You know that. You helped me pick out my prom dress and then went with me to return it after he stood me up."

"Yes. I remember. I just thought…"

"What?" Pausing, Maggie peered at her.

"Nothing. My memory of those days is kind of foggy. I had a lot on my mind, what with your daddy's illness and all."

Maggie slipped an arm around her mother's

shoulders and gave her a quick squeeze. "I know. I'm sorry you had to worry about me so much then, too. You had a lot on your plate." She glanced at the sink. "Speaking of plates, why don't I help you finish the dishes before we go join the boys?"

Smiling wistfully, Faye agreed. "Okay. I guess I should be thankful you adopted a dog for Mark's playmate instead of taming a raccoon."

"Or a skunk," Maggie teased. "Good thing my job teaches me to avoid making pets of my patients. Some of those baby animals are adorable."

"Not as adorable as my grandson."

Despite herself, Maggie silently added, *Or his daddy.*

When Flint had first shown up at the compound, every nerve in her body insisted he was nothing but trouble. Then, after he'd shoved her out of the line of fire, she simply credited his actions to his training and combat experience. But when he'd tracked her into the woods after the accident and offered comfort, she lost her defensive edge. Fortifications she'd erected around her tender heart had been breached. Cracked. Left crumbling.

She didn't love Flint, she argued. Not the way she once had. And yet there was something there. Something she couldn't quite put her finger on.

Something almost as scary as the apparent threats to her continued safety and well-being.

And that of her son. Their son: hers and Flint's. An innocent child caught between the past and the present, whose future might be in jeopardy because of the sins of his parents.

Maggie finally understood why her own family had tried so hard to keep her away from Flint.

Too bad their efforts had come too late.

FIVE

Flint's division headquarters was in Mammoth Spring and included six counties, meaning he wouldn't normally have been sent to officially visit Maggie's rehab center if Captain Lang hadn't made it a priority.

The sheriff had graciously agreed to keep an eye on her when chores on his great-grandparents' farm kept Flint too busy. The place had really deteriorated while he was away. No sooner did he repair one thing than another broke. He'd finished nailing down the leaky barn roof and then the tractor had refused to start so he could use it to restack bales of hay.

Flint saw only one viable solution. He'd have to convince the elderly couple to stop farming. A successful operation needed a lot more supervision and daily care than he was able to give it. Ira could hire his hay cut and baled, but without good cattle management he'd go deeper in debt every year, and the stubborn old man insisted on keeping all the records himself.

Using a rag to wipe black grease off his hands, Flint headed for the house.

Bess met him at the back door with a smile. "Good. I was just coming to get you. Lunch is ready."

"Okay. Let me wash up first." Although she was in her eighties, Bess still had the kind of energy and zest for life Flint remembered from his youth. She wore her gray hair in a long braid and perched her glasses on the end of her nose to peer over them even though they were bifocals.

It had been a bit of a shock to return and find such big changes in everything else. The house was in better shape than the outbuildings, but not by much. It needed painting as well as several new sections of chimney pipe to safely vent the wood-burning stove. Flint had already suggested they add propane heaters and had had his idea totally rejected, even after offering to pay for the tank and installation.

Still pondering the immense task of fixing the old house, he joined the older couple at the kitchen table. Ira had always been the one to say a prayer of thanks for the food, but since Flint had returned, Bess had begun asking him to do it.

He slid his chair up to the table and noted that Ira was already eating. "Sorry I'm late. I didn't want to show up with tractor grease under my nails. Did you say grace, Papaw?"

The old man's rheumy, greenish eyes were focused on the distance and he was eating as if by habit rather than for enjoyment the way he used to.

"He was starving," Bess said, "so we started without you. Gotta keep my hungry husband happy."

"No problem." Flint followed by a quick bow of his head and a soft "Amen."

"So, did you get the roof nailed down good?"

He met her questioning gaze with one of his own. "Uh-huh. How long has it been since Papaw ran that tractor? It's a mess. I had to drain the fuel and clean the filters before it would do more than cough a few times. It's running rough now, but at least it's running."

"We haven't had a lot of need for our own machinery lately," Bess said. "We hire most things done. That's sensible at our age."

Glancing at Ira as she spoke, Flint waited for some sign of agreement. What he got, instead, was a muttered curse, something the confused old man would never have done if he'd been in his right mind.

"I'll be glad to do whatever I can on my days off," Flint said, "but you really need more help around here than that."

"Don't need nothin' from nobody," Ira mumbled gruffly.

Well, at least he's speaking, Flint thought, wondering how to best keep him engaged. This kind of attitude, let alone peppered with bad language, was not like the man he'd idolized from the moment his great-grandparents took him in and provided a stable home.

"You two have always looked out for others. It's time we repaid you."

"If it needs doin' I'll take care of it," Ira insisted. He pushed to his feet, leaning on the edge of the table for support. "Don't need no interference from you or anybody else."

Bess reached toward Flint and touched his hand as her husband did his best to storm off despite stiff knees and hips. "Don't pay him any mind. He's just achin' more with winter comin' on," she said. "He gets this way when he's hurting bad."

"What does his doctor say?"

She chuckled, eyes twinkling. "Not much other than hello when we see him in church. Your papaw hasn't been to a doctor in a coon's age."

"Probably more like an elephant's age," Flint countered with a shake of his head. "It's probably not safe to let him continue to drive, either. What if he gets lost?"

"He won't. We got that GPS thingie on the new pickup."

"I saw it under a tarp in the barn. Can't you do something about getting him to see a doctor?"

"Well, I suppose you and I could try to stuff him in a feed sack and deliver him to the doc that way, but he'd be plenty mad when we let him out." She sobered. "I've done my best to talk him into seeing our family doctor. It's no use. Ira just gets upset, like now, and storms off. I suspect he'd be in a better mood if he'd take something for his pain, but he won't touch a pill. Not even aspirin."

"Because of my mother?"

"And her mother before her."

Signing, Flint clasped Bess's thin hand, taking care not to squeeze the distended knuckles. "Just because addiction happens to one person in a family, that doesn't mean the rest of us are doomed."

"I know." Bess's eyes were misted. "We did our best with our daughter. Even helped her raise your mama. But drugs got 'em both before they were old enough to vote. I think Ira blames himself."

"That's ridiculous."

Bess snorted. "Warn me if you ever decide to say that to his face, okay? I wanna be far, far away."

Far away? Been there, done that, Flint thought,

and look what it got me. The loving old couple who kept me from going wrong as a teenager are failing, the farm is in ruin and Maggie has made a new life without me.

Not that it made sense to think the love of his life would have waited for him. Their families had both been dead set against their romance, so what could he expect?

That introspection brought him to ask something else that had been bothering him. "You know just about everybody in town over the age of thirty. Do you think Missy and Sonny Dodd could be dangerous?"

Bess smirked. "Well, Missy might talk a body to death, but otherwise they're mostly blowin' smoke."

"What about Elwood Witherspoon?"

Her fingers pressed over her lips, and her eyes widened. "Why do you ask?"

"Just wondering. My captain mentioned Elwood. Other wardens have come up against him—when they can find him—and they say he's a real piece of work."

"I haven't seen Elwood to speak to for years. Sorry."

Frowning, Flint studied her expression. "Are you all right?"

"Fine."

If she hadn't been casting worried glances through the door into the living room and looking as if she were about to pass out, Flint might have accepted her statement without reservations. He wasn't quite through eating but started to rise when she did. "Want me to help you clean up?"

"No, no. I'm used to doin' kitchen chores. You finish your sandwich, then go back and tinker with that old tractor. In spite of what Ira says, I know this place needs a lot of TLC."

"Have you ever thought of moving, maybe into assisted living?" Flint ventured.

Bess fumbled a plate and it shattered against the edge of the sink. "Mercy, no. Whatever gave you such a crazy idea?"

"It would make your life much easier. Here. Let me help you clean that up."

She flapped her hands as if shooing a pesky fly. "No need. I can handle my own kitchen, and your grandpa can take care of this farm, okay?"

"Okay. Sorry I mentioned it." He bent to kiss her cheek. "If you need me I'll be in the barn."

He'd donned a jacket and was easing the back door closed behind him when he heard his great-grandmother gasp. Ira's raised voice carried. "See? What'd I tell you. He wants our farm. Him and that hussy who's got him all befuddled again."

"That's pure nonsense."

Flint was torn between a desire to barge in and refute the claim and the knowledge that his best recourse would be to let his actions prove him innocent. He loved those two old people more than anything. Their health was deteriorating. It was natural for them to worry about their future and to want to cling to the past, to try to maintain the same lifestyle they'd enjoyed for so many years.

He eased the door shut all the way. There was a lot to be said for a good old-fashioned rut. At this point in his life Flint felt more like an outsider than ever. He'd been fatherless for as long as he could remember, neglected and then orphaned, and had failed to find direction or purpose in the military. If he hadn't gotten Bess's letter begging for his help, he didn't know where he'd have ended up. Certainly not in Serenity, where past mistakes kept staring him in the face.

That was the crux of his unrest, he decided. There were too many memories, too many disappointments, lurking around every corner. And speaking of lurking, he hadn't heard a word from the sheriff in days. It was time to check with him for an update and dig deeper into reports of Elwood's poaching.

Flint palmed his cell phone and stared at it. Phoning Sheriff Allgood was the sensible thing to do. But if he called Maggie he could get her input, as well. Besides, he admitted with a wry smile, he wanted to hear her voice again. To have her personally assure him she was all right.

He punched in the number of the sanctuary.

Nobody picked up. He left a brief message on Maggie's answering machine, promising himself he'd try again later, then went back to work in the barn.

After supper, Flint tried to phone her for the fifth time. Still no answer. The hair on the back of his neck prickled. As far as he knew, Maggie had no hired help, relying on volunteer labor in order to keep costs down. Therefore, she should be home. Even if she'd left the compound to run errands, she was bound to check her answering machine occasionally.

So, now what? He was getting more and more worried. If he failed to reach her soon, he'd have to either contact the sheriff and ask him to send someone to investigate, or make the trip to Maggie's himself. Alerting law enforcement for nothing wasn't a good idea. Then again, neither was showing up at her place repeatedly with the excuse of looking for her uncle.

Disgusted, Flint accepted the inevitable. He had to be the one to go have a look-see. If things went well, it might not be necessary to let anyone else know he was even slightly concerned.

He grabbed his jacket and handgun on his way to the door and called to his grandmother, "I have to go out. Be back soon."

If she replied before the door slammed, Flint didn't hear. He was loping toward the AGFC truck, and the faster he moved, the more his heart kept pace.

"I'll feel really stupid if I get there and Maggie's fine," he told himself. That warning did nothing to slow him. He'd much rather be thought a fool than find out later that Maggie *wasn't* fine.

Sunset had brought with it a sense of impending winter. Maggie shivered. The air was damp and chilly, the last brown leaves barely clinging to myriad oaks, sycamores and other native floras. Only the cedars remained green.

She'd left Mark in the house with Wolfie while she tended to her evening chores right outside. Given the dropping temperatures, it was necessary to provide extra bedding for her larger patients and perhaps move some of the smaller cages under better cover.

The niggling sense that she was being watched made Maggie's skin prickle. She kept looking over her shoulder as she worked, seeing nothing out of the ordinary, yet convinced she wasn't alone.

Pulling off flakes of bedding hay, she piled them on a yard cart. Wind whipped loose stem fragments from the pile and swirled them high. Maggie sneezed once, twice, then drew breath to repeat. With her chin lifted she had a different view of her surroundings and thought she saw something moving in the forest.

"Of course I did," she muttered. "Achoo! Stuff out there blows around just like my hay." Which was not entirely true. Any lightweight vegetation would still be soggy from the recent rain. Her stored hay, on the other hand, was dry and more easily disturbed.

Most of the outdoor pens were adjacent to the house, while the smallest cages found protection in the barn. Maggie was passing a window that was low enough to let her peek in to check on Mark, so she paused. He and the dog were playing catch. That wasn't an approved activity for inside, but they were quiet and happy. As long as the boy remembered to keep his tosses low, she wasn't going to interfere.

A deep, distant howl stood the hairs on Maggie's neck on end. She whirled, facing the direction of the sound just in time to hear an answering echo about twenty degrees east of the first. Listening intently, she held her breath. Higher-pitched yips joined the elongated cries that were so intense, so primal, they infiltrated her most basic senses. Adults and pups. Only *not* coyotes. What was a wolf pack doing in the Ozarks?

Instinct made Maggie spin back around. For an instant she forgot she'd been watching her son, so when she came practically nose-to-nose with Wolfie on the other side of the glass, she almost screamed.

The dog pawed at the window, panting until it was steamy. "You hear them, too, don't you?" His ears perked. He cocked his head. "Take it easy. It's okay, boy."

The howls seemed to be getting closer. Maggie cast around for a defensive weapon. The only thing handy was a pitchfork. She reached for the handle. Stumbled over a wheel of the yard cart. Felt herself falling.

She missed catching hold of anything to break her fall and went down hard. In the midst of her useless flailing, she finally did scream.

Glass cracked and broke above her. Maggie covered her head with her arms, letting her jacket take most of the punishment from the falling shards.

There had been no shots this time. She was certain of it. So what…?

Something landed beside her with a soft thud and she knew instantly what had happened. This was the second time Wolfie had breached a closed window. The first time had been when Mark was a toddler and there had been a stray dog in the yard.

Maggie levered herself up just in time to see her enormous dog bound over the cart and disappear into the thick forest. "Wolfie! No!

"Wolfie, come." She started to get to her feet. Looked down at her hands. And saw blood.

SIX

The first thing Flint noticed as he slowly pulled into Maggie's driveway was her. She was pacing the porch and looked beside herself. Her eyes were wide, her hair flyaway. When she ran straight to him instead of holding her ground, he knew something was terribly wrong. "Why didn't you answer your phone? Did you leave it in the house again?"

She latched on to the sleeve of his jacket as soon as he stepped out of the truck. "You have to help me."

"Okay. What's wrong?"

Gesturing wildly, she indicated the woods at the edge of the compound. "Wolves. I heard them."

"Did they approach? Menace you in any way?"

"No, but—"

"Then go back in the house. I'll check your pens."

"It's not that."

As her grip tightened, Flint glanced down. Was that a trace of blood on the cuff of her jacket? His breath caught. "Are you hurt?"

"No. Not me, Wolfie. He crashed through a window and ran off. If the pack spots him, they'll kill him. He won't be able to fight them all."

Flint took a step forward. "Okay. I'll radio a report and board up your window while we wait for more help."

The noise she made was half exasperation, half anger. As soon as he was through contacting his partner, she said, "I nailed a board over the window myself. I called the sheriff, too, but he said there was nothing he could do about a runaway dog."

"Why didn't you call Game and Fish?"

When Maggie rolled her eyes, he had his answer.

"I get it. You'd rather have your dog die than ask me for anything."

"No! I never said that. I left a message on the answering machine at your office."

Flint was penitent. "Right. It's Saturday. Sorry." He eyed the porch. "Why don't we go wait inside?"

Her "No!" was so forceful he stepped back, hands raised as if he were being robbed at gunpoint. "Okay, okay. I'll look around out here and listen for more howling after I call and ask somebody to bring me an ATV." He studied her. "Will that do?"

"I guess it'll have to."

They stepped off the porch together. He'd dealt with plenty of anxious people in the course of his duties, but Maggie's case was extreme. Maybe if he could distract her she'd be more tractable. "Is your kid at your mother's today?"

She stopped in her tracks. "No. Why?"

"Because that's where he was when you had that wreck," Flint said.

"Only because we were being shot at when he got out of school," she countered. "I take good care of him."

"I'm sure you do." He took time to rephrase his query. "I was asking because I wanted to know if you were free to help me start to trail your dog instead of waiting for wheels."

"Oh." Maggie cast a brief glance at the house. "No. That's why I needed help. I can't leave Mark here all by himself."

"Understood." Flint was grabbing gear out of his truck and loading a small backpack. "Okay. Point me in the right direction."

"This way."

As he followed her across the yard and past the broken window, he was listening intently. Except for the occasional birdcall and rustling of squirrels among the dry leaves aloft, nothing broke the rural silence.

Maggie stopped at the edge of the cleared land and pointed. "He went through here, on the deer trail. After that I have no idea."

Crouching, Flint touched a fingertip to a darker spot on the ground. Wolfie was leaving a trail. Of blood. All the more reason for wolves to attack him.

As he stood, Flint realized from Maggie's expression that she had come to the same disturbing conclusion.

"I'll do my best to track him down for you," he promised. "When my partner gets here, point him in this direction. He can use GPS to find me."

"I will."

The clenching of her slim fingers made him want to cover her clasped hands with his and offer more tangible comfort. He refrained. All he had to do to convince himself it was a bad idea was to remember the awkwardness after her accident. The adverse effect of that closeness, although innocent, lingered. And when she'd grabbed his forearm a few minutes ago, every one of his nerves tingled.

Nevertheless, Flint stood stock-still. Staring into her eyes. Drowning in their blue-water depths.

Maggie didn't move, either. Time stopped.

Finally, Flint shouldered his pack, turned and started into the forest without another word. He didn't look back until he heard Maggie call, "I'll pray for you."

Was that something new or had she remembered him in prayer while he was away, too? He had often prayed for her during the time they were apart, at least when he wasn't being distracted by the fight to stay alive. Every time he lost a comrade in combat, it magnified how alone he really was.

Now he was back with the remnant of his family and the folks he'd known while growing up, yet there were times when he felt more alone *now* than he had when he was half a world away.

Sighing, he slowed to check the trail of intermittent blood drops, then straightened and paused to listen, expecting howling. Instead, he heard a distant shout. *Maggie?* His heart threatened to pound right out of his chest until his radio crackled. The ATV had arrived already and was being unloaded.

Gathering himself so he wouldn't sound breathless, he keyed his mic. "This is Crawford. Wait for me at the house. I'll be right back."

That decision would probably displease Maggie, but it couldn't be helped. Better to have wheels and make good time than to fail because of darkness. The headlights on the four-wheel-drive vehicle would help a lot as the sun set.

Flint grabbed the shoulder straps of the pack and began to jog. The chances that Maggie would have taken his advice and gone into the house were slim to none. She was bound to be waiting, ready to chew him out for not finding her injured dog.

He broke from the woods and kept going. There she was. And more beautiful than ever, with a wildness about her that made her seem a part of the mountains they both loved. She'd pulled her jacket tightly around her and was facing into the wind, her hair lifting on the breeze.

Flint slowed to a brisk walk and approached. His jaw muscles clenched as he assessed his errant feelings. Above all, it was imperative he squelch any emotional links to Maggie Morgan.

He'd been rejected by her once.

Once was enough.

Maggie had immediately recognized Warden Samson when he pulled up. Cautioning Mark to stay inside while she went to brief the warden, she'd hurried down the porch steps.

"Flint—I mean Warden Crawford—went after my dog."

The dark-haired young agent frowned at her. "Yeah. I know. He contacted me."

"Did he find him?" Her hopes soared until the warden shook his head. "I heard a pack of wolves."

"Aren't any wolves in Arkansas," Samson countered, putting out ramps and unloading the

ATV from the back of his pickup. "Only thing I've seen around here that looked like one is that dog of yours." He smiled. "Maybe he's lookin' for kin."

"Better his than mine," she said wryly. "Crawford's on foot. He said to use GPS to meet up with him."

"No need." Samson gestured with his chin. "Here he comes."

Before she could speak, Flint began to explain. "I followed the dog as far as Lick Creek. I'll drive back and pick up the trail where I left off."

"Want me to hang around here?" the other warden asked.

"Not unless you feel like getting in trouble, too."

Samson grinned. "We could call it public service."

Maggie suddenly understood what the men were saying. Flint was out there on his own time, with borrowed equipment, looking for a domestic animal, when that wasn't included in his regular duties. Involving a partner just made the infraction worse.

"He was bleeding," Maggie offered, so thankful she didn't know how to express it. "Is that how you tracked him?"

"Partly. It's hard to tell how badly he's hurt without knowing how fast he's traveling. At least he was still on the move when he got to the creek."

"Maybe he'll lay up in the water and you'll find him soon."

"Maybe." Flint glanced at the sky. "Gotta go. I'm losing daylight."

The other warden waved and climbed into his own truck as Flint gunned the ATV engine and sped off.

"Please, God," Maggie whispered. "Help him."

She was familiar enough with injured animals to know they would "go to ground" if they felt unable to continue. The icy creek water would help Wolfie slow his bleeding if it was out of control. The downside was the chance that he'd chill his body too much and go into hypothermia. That could kill him, too, if he wasn't found in time.

Biting her lip to squelch tears, she turned and started back to the house, back to her waiting son. The right thing to do was tell him the truth, although she hated the idea. Children were tenderhearted. They took losses hard.

With loss on her mind, Maggie pictured Flint. How was she going to keep her sanity when she kept seeing him? Didn't he know how hard it was for her? Didn't he care?

Perhaps this was his way of punishing her, she mused, rejecting the idea only partially. Whether he meant to or not, his continued presence was adding to her anguish like a knife through her heart.

She climbed the steps and opened her front door to greet her anxious son. One thing was certain. Although she thought her pain was bad now, the future promised to be much worse.

Opening her arms to Mark, she dropped to one knee and held him close. She must not weep. Not now. Not ever. She had to maintain a strong, capable image for the sake of her little boy.

"Where's Wolfie?" he asked.

Maggie set him away and met his inquiring gaze with what she hoped was assurance. "The game warden is out looking for him."

"Why doesn't he just come home?"

That was an excellent question, one she didn't want to answer. Nevertheless, it was necessary if she was to keep the child's trust.

"Wolfie hurt himself when he broke the glass in the window," Maggie said tenderly. "Sometimes, when animals get hurt, they go hide instead of looking for help."

"But he loves us."

"Yes, he does. And we love him, too." She paused, deciding how blunt to be. "But sometimes love isn't enough."

"Uh-uh," Mark insisted. "Jesus loves us and that's enough."

"True." It was all Maggie could do to fight the tears gathering behind her lashes. No wonder scripture instructed believers to "come as a little child." The faith of children put adults to shame, herself included.

"Let's pray for Wolfie," Mark said.

What would happen to his faith if the dog never came home? she wondered. How could she protect his tender heart from the kinds of deep disappointments she had experienced?

"You know," Maggie told him gently, "sometimes God decides that what was asked for isn't best, so He doesn't give it to us."

"Okay." He smiled.

"Okay?"

"Sure." The smile grew to a grin. "I trust Jesus. Don't you?"

The innocent question echoed in Maggie's heart. She did trust Him. After all, her commitment to her Christian faith had been reaffirmed when she reached her lowest point just before Mark was born. Had she forgotten how cherished and loved she'd felt then? Had her sense of belonging waned as life had sped by?

There was only one thing to do. Kneeling beside her son, she folded her hands, bowed her head and joined him in praying for the welfare of a simple dog.

And while she did so, she silently added thanks for everything the Lord had given her and asked forgiveness for her lack of faith.

Then, as if back where she'd begun, she also

asked for the wisdom to know what to tell Mark if Wolfie never came home to them.

The irony of that struck her with dismay. How could she hope to lead her son when he was the one leading her?

Maggie clamped her hands together more tightly as her mind and heart filled with a different unspoken prayer. Despite knowing it was impossible, she wanted to go back to her teenage years and take up where she and Flint had left off.

This time, tears did begin to fall.

Mark said, "Amen," stood and wrapped his little arms around her neck, then leaned closer to whisper, "Don't cry, Mama. I prayed for you, too."

Flint had dismounted periodically to make sure he hadn't lost the trail. Since the last rain, the forest floor had remained damp, so tracks were easier to spot, particularly along the creek banks.

Scowling, he bent for a closer look. There were large canine tracks, all right. There were also waffle imprints left by hiking boots that overlapped them. Tensing, he rested his palm against the grip of his pistol. This wasn't public land, so what was the person in boots doing out here? Moreover, why was he apparently trailing the dog?

It was easy for Flint to assume the paw prints he'd been following belonged to Maggie's pet. If there had been an actual wolf pack roaming the area, there would be more than one set of tracks and the sizes would vary.

He heard a distinct whimper. Froze. Listened. There it was again!

Still cautious, Flint left the ATV and began to work his way toward the sounds. The closer he got, the more the whining increased, leading him to suspect he was approaching a domestic animal. A wild one would have quieted in order to hide from a human.

There was a splashing sound from the creek. A series of yips, then a deep bark. Flint picked up his pace. That was no wolf. That was Maggie's dog.

The moment they set eyes on each other, Wolfie lowered his head, stuck his rear up in the air and wagged his bushy tail.

Flint grinned. "You sure gave us a scare." He paused and patted his thigh. "Come here. Let me look at you."

Wolfie was wiggling side to side but not approaching. As Flint drew closer he could see why. The dog was tied to a tree with a frayed piece of rope. Moreover, it looked as if somebody had tried to bandage his bleeding paw.

"Well, well, well. What do we have here? Looks like somebody tried to help you." A quick scan of the neighboring terrain showed no sign of the Good Samaritan.

Flint bent to inspect the injury and saw more blood in the icy creek water. "You should have had sense enough to leave the bandage alone," Flint said, gathering up the loosened strip of cloth and rinsing it in the running stream before untying the rope. To be on the safe side, he kept hold of it and led Wolfie slowly back to the ATV.

"Okay. Sit. I have to use the radio." Realizing he was making polite conversation with a dog, Flint chuckled. He was getting as bad as Maggie.

"Samson, this is Crawford. I have the dog and I'm bringing him in."

"Good," the other warden replied. "Want me to go back and tell Maggie or will you do it?"

Truth to tell, Flint wished he could pass Wolfie off on his fellow warden and not go back to Maggie's at all, but the injured animal came first. "I'll do it. Thanks for your help."

"Don't mention it. And I mean that literally— don't mention it." He was laughing when Flint signed off.

Reaching down, Flint scratched behind the dog's ears and down his broad back until Wolfie dropped to the ground in apparent ecstasy. As Flint switched to a tummy rub, he checked the injured paw. Pressure stopped the bleeding, but as soon as he let go it resumed.

"I need to put your bandage back on, boy," Flint said softly. "Here we go. That's it. Good boy."

The strip of cloth was barely long enough for the job, but it stuck to itself pretty well now that it was wet. Wondering how he'd keep it there while they rode back to Maggie, Flint thought of his gloves. The cuff of one of them might just do the trick, assuming he could keep the dog from pulling it off and having it for supper.

He eyed his patient. "Too bad you're so big. I could tuck something like a hurt rabbit inside my jacket."

Picturing himself trying that with all hundred and some pounds of Wolfie, he chuckled. "Let's try a calf carry instead. I'll be the cowboy."

Flint swung astride the ATV, lifted Wolfie and slung him across the seat in front of him, head on one side, tail on the other, the way a wrangler would transport a weak calf. The dog wasn't happy being treated that way.

"No. Stay," Flint ordered. To his surprise, Wolfie quit wiggling, sighed and started to relax, even allowing his rescuer to slip a glove over the bandage on his sore paw. That made carrying him easier but was not a good sign overall because it might mean he was showing fatigue from blood loss.

It wasn't until they were on their way that Flint remembered that in his haste to get medical treatment for his patient he'd forgotten to notify Maggie. His cell phone was zipped inside a jacket pocket and right now it was all he could do to keep the dog balanced as well as steer.

"She'll have to wait," he told himself, accelerating slowly. "We'll be there in no time."

The weary dog looked up at him with such expressive eyes Flint continued to reassure him with a friendly tone. "I promise, okay? Ten minutes, tops."

Wolfie's broad black nose twitched. His head lifted a little more. His lips curled back and quivered as he began to stare into the darkening depths of the forest.

Flint felt the dog's growl rather than heard it over the roar of the engine. Since there was no way he could drive and use a cell phone, there was certainly no way he could safely draw a gun. Therefore, he could either run for it or make a stand right here and take the chance the poor dog would survive the delay.

A shot echoed. That simplified his decision. *Run.*

He hunched low over the front of the small vehicle, using his upper torso to help hold Wolfie in place, then gave the ATV more gas. A lot more gas. Whoever or whatever was lurking in ambush would never be able to overtake them on foot. All Flint had to do was keep from hitting a tree or dropping a wheel into a hidden depression and sending them both flying, and they'd survive.

Beneath his chest, he began to sense a lack of tension. "Hang in there, Wolfie," he said. "Don't give up on me now. We're almost home." The dog didn't move. Didn't struggle anymore.

Flint held his own breath. *No, not now. Not when we're so close to Maggie.*

He broke from the forest into a clearing. The sanctuary compound lay just ahead.

They'd made it.

Or had they?

SEVEN

The roaring rumble of the small engine drew Maggie out onto the front porch. When Mark tried to follow, she stopped him. "Stay in the house where it's warm, honey. I'll be right back."

"But, Mama—"

"No. I said stay in there."

His muffled reply as she shut the door sounded close enough to "Yes, ma'am" to be acceptable.

Fingers pressed to her lips, she watched the ATV speed across the yard and slide to a stop. She ran to meet it. "Is he...?"

"I thought I might have lost him, but he perked up when he heard your voice just now," Flint said, dismounting and helping her lift the semi-limp dog.

Maggie had latched on to Wolfie's head and shoulders and was relieved when he began trying to lick her face. She would have loved to carry him into the house but knew better than to suggest it while Mark was present.

"Where do you want me to put him?" Flint asked.

"I don't know. Um, I suppose around back. I can make him a bed of straw and watch him until the vet can drive over." She eyed the glove. "How badly is he hurt?"

"He'd be better if he hadn't pulled off his bandage and started the bleeding again."

"Thanks for the first aid."

It surprised her to see Flint shaking his head. "Don't thank me. Somebody else wrapped his paw and tied him to a tree. I suppose they figured you'd be able to locate him easier that way."

"Who?"

"Beats me. I saw boot tracks in the mud along the creek bank near where he was tied." Flint sobered. "At least one other person had been out there, maybe more. I'd just decided the area was secure when Wolfie sensed something and started to growl."

"Did you spot anybody?"

"No. But I trusted the dog's instincts. Good thing, too. We were heading back when I heard a shot."

"Were they aiming at you?" Maggie could tell he suspected so but was trying to play down the danger.

"Possibly." Flint shrugged one shoulder. "I decided we'd better head back here on the double just in case. Better to play it safe."

"Absolutely." Maggie had already been anxious. Now she began trembling so badly she had trouble holding up her end of the dog. Thankfully, Flint stepped up to cradle the full weight.

"Sorry," she said. "It's been a rough day."

Light from the single bulb on the porch cast long shadows that didn't extend around the side of the house. Flint pointed with his chin. "I know I outran that shooter, so how about turning on a few more lights? I'll need to see where I'm going."

"Yes. Right." She turned back just as the front door burst open. Before she could catch her little boy, he was down the steps and racing barefoot toward his injured pet.

"Wolfie!"

Maggie screeched, "No!" but it was too late. Mark had reached Flint and the dog.

Flint grinned and lowered the squirming dog to the ground, kneeling beside him while the child buried his face in the long, thick fur and sobbed audibly.

The sight of father and son together tore at Maggie's heart. Flint had apparently not figured things out yet, but he soon would, particularly once Mark looked at him with those Crawford-green eyes.

What could she do? How could she soften the blow? And how in the world was she going to keep Flint from showing anger in front of the impressionable child?

Standing close by and looking down on them, Maggie wondered if she should try to intervene. Even if she scooped up Mark and hurried him back to the house, Flint was sure to follow with the dog. Would that be so bad? It would not only be safer, but it beat letting her son linger in the yard when he was wearing nothing but pajamas.

It was time to clear the air. Get the drama over with and take the consequences. She'd dreaded this day for years, yet it was now being forced on her.

Silently, she stripped off her own jacket and wrapped it around the child while praying, "Father, give me strength."

As she turned Mark and lifted him, she pressed his head to her shoulder to temporarily hide his face. "All right," she said with a noisy sigh. "Let's all go in the house and keep warm while I phone the vet."

"The dog, too?" Flint asked.

"Yes. Can you manage him by yourself?"

"Sure. No problem. Now that he's wide-awake I can always put him down for a minute if he causes too much trouble."

Trouble? she mused. Ha! If he thought the dog was the only thing going to cause trouble tonight, he was in for a real shock. Her stomach tied in knots. No matter how many times she had imagined this confrontation or rehearsed it in her mind, she wasn't ready. Not even close.

The front door stood open. This was her last chance to postpone Flint's rude awakening. If she shouldered in ahead of him and shooed her son away…

No. That was not only wrong, but it was cowardly. Flint was the one who had left her, not the other way around. His guilt was more than equal to hers. As he was about to find out.

Pausing at the threshold, Flint eased Wolfie down onto his remaining three good paws. He'd done his duty. He'd found Maggie's dog and brought him home. The most sensible action now would be to bid her good-night and drive away. But what if she needed more help? Suppose she failed to get hold of the vet she'd mentioned? What then?

He couldn't leave. Not yet. He straightened and stood tall, watching the dog limp into the main room and plop down on a small rug near the fireplace.

Maggie was fussing over the little boy, making motherly noises about slippers and a robe while the child tried to dodge past her to return to his pet. Flint had shut the door and was about to praise her for being a good mama when he caught his first clear glimpse of the child's face.

The sight was literally staggering. His spine

hit the doorjamb. His jaw hung slack. Words failed him. He couldn't tear his gaze away. It felt as though he were looking into a mirror over fifteen years ago and seeing his own reflection.

Stunned, mute, he studied Mark. This was Maggie's boy? How could they look so much alike? They had only once lost control. Why hadn't she said something to him back then? Had she been so ashamed to have consorted with a Crawford that she'd tried to hide the truth from everybody?

Mark ducked past his mother and raced back to the dog, hitting his knees and gently hugging Wolfie's neck. Only then did Flint manage to look at Maggie. Tears were streaming down her cheeks. Her lips were trembling.

She met his questioning gaze and mouthed, *I'm sorry.*

Flint nodded. His jaw clamped shut. There was still no adequate way to express his emotional upheaval short of stammering incoherently and making a worse fool of himself. No wonder so many people had grinned at him after he'd returned to Serenity. They knew something he didn't. Their amusement at his expense was infuriating.

She took a tentative step closer to him. "I'm so sorry. I know I should have said something when you first came back, but…"

He wanted to shout at her. To berate her for so

many omissions. To ask if she'd ever have owned up to the boy's parentage if he hadn't shown up again. But before he could decide where and how to begin, Mark called, "Mama! Look."

Both adults pivoted toward the anxious child. He was cradling the hurt paw in his hands as blood dripped through his tiny fingers.

Maggie was the first to respond. She grabbed the paw and squeezed the edges just enough to slow the bleeding, then cast around, apparently looking for something with which to fashion a temporary bandage.

"Where's your first aid kit?" Flint demanded.

"Outside with the other animal supplies. There's a towel in the kitchen." She indicated a doorway, then looked to her son. "Mark, honey, go wash your hands and bring Mommy a clean towel, okay?"

Instead of obeying, the boy stared at his red-dened fingers and whimpered.

Flint strode into the kitchen, pulled several paper towels from a roll, wet one and grabbed a dry dish towel. Operating as if back in combat, he returned to the living room and thrust the towel at Maggie before crouching beside her to wipe the child's hands.

He then shoved the used paper towels at Maggie, edged her aside, took a firm hold of the dog's paw and said, "Go call your vet. And tell him to hurry. I'm not staying any longer than I have to."

Given his uneasiness, Flint figured his best option was to concentrate on the task at hand and put everything else out of his mind. For now at any rate.

He'd almost succeeded when the little sandy-haired boy trained big green eyes on him and said, "Thank you for saving my dog, mister."

"You're welcome."

That would have been the end of Flint's communication if Mark had not gotten up and wrapped his little arms tightly around Flint's neck.

Long seconds passed. Flint was astounded when his vision misted. He shifted his hold on the dog enough to free one arm and wrap it gently around his son.

Then he laid his face against Mark's shoulder, mirroring the child's stance, and closed his eyes.

Maggie could hardly function, let alone speak coherently, when the veterinarian's answering machine picked up her call. She knew she was babbling instead of giving her usual concise report of conditions, but she couldn't help herself.

A voice came on the line halfway through her first convoluted sentence. "Is this Maggie Morgan?"

"Yes!"

"I can hardly understand you. Calm down. Tell me what's wrong."

"Wolfie's hurt. His paw is bleeding something awful."

"You know how vascular extremities are. Have you applied pressure?"

She glanced over at the tableau on the hearth rug. It was so touching, so tender, she could barely speak until she looked away. "Yes. But every time we let go it starts bleeding again."

"I can't stitch a dog's pad. It won't hold. Besides, it needs to heal from the inside out. How did it happen?"

"He jumped through a window."

"A closed window? Again?"

Realizing she was nodding instead of answering verbally, Maggie gave a delayed "Yes."

"All right. I'll be right over. He may have other injuries as well as the foot. In the meantime, keep him quiet and keep putting pressure on the cut you can see."

"Okay. Thanks."

As she ended the call, she refocused on Flint. He had parted from Mark and was encouraging the boy to help him comfort Wolfie. Both father and son had their heads bowed. Mark's open hands rested on the dog's head while Flint continued to grip the paw.

Maggie heard her son's "Amen" before he went on to inform Flint that he was the answer to an earlier prayer. "Mama didn't want to pray for Wolfie, but I did." Mark beamed at the man. "And you found him."

"It's my job to help hurt animals and protect the forest and lakes," Flint explained.

"That's what I wanna do when I grow up."

In other words, they had only just met and already Mark wanted to be exactly like his daddy. Maggie tried to swallow the dry lump in her throat and failed. She coughed. Flint glanced up. Any fondness vanished as soon as he focused on her and asked, "Vet's on his way?"

"Yes. Greg said he'd be here ASAP."

"Greg Gogerty? I remember hearing that he was practicing around here. He's Miss Inez's grandson, right?"

"Yes. He treats both large and small animals."

A sardonic chuckle from Flint surprised her until he explained, "I hope he has some hefty assistants. As I recall, Greg was a scrawny little guy."

She wanted to snap back with *So were you* but refrained. No use antagonizing Flint, particularly since he seemed to be handling his meeting with his son far better than expected. Maggie was intensely grateful. She'd much rather take the brunt of the man's understandable anger than have it foisted on her innocent child.

"I'm sure Greg can handle Wolfie," she said. "They know each other. This isn't the first time that dog has sailed through glass."

"I sure hope it's the last," Flint said. "I'd expect him to be smarter than that."

"He's just very protective. I guess he thought the wolves were sneaking up on me."

"You're sticking with that story?"

Her brow knitted. "What's that supposed to mean?"

"Look. I didn't mind searching for your dog while I was off duty. But if you intend to send me on a wild-goose chase, you're going to have to come up with something more believable than wolves."

"I *heard* them," she insisted.

"Uh-huh. Then why didn't I see a single track?"

Maggie didn't have a ready answer. She certainly wasn't going to suggest that perhaps he lacked skill. "How should I know? Wolfie was lost, just like I said, wasn't he?"

"In a manner of speaking. I told you somebody had already found him. What I don't understand is why they didn't bring him back to you then."

"Maybe they were afraid to let him walk."

"And maybe he was bait to lure me out there so they could take more potshots at me."

"That's crazy!" She threw her hands up in frustration.

"From where I stand, it seems plausible. It was your story and your dog."

"I'd never purposely hurt any animal, especially not one who's like a member of my family."

"Maybe not. But I can see you taking advantage of an accident."

Astonished, she fisted her hands on her hips. "Why in the world would I do that?"

Instead of answering in so many words, Flint turned to glance at his son and heard Mark whispering to the injured dog. Suddenly Maggie understood. He actually believed she'd abuse one of God's creatures in order to preserve her secret. How *dare* he?

The realization stunned her. "How can you think so little of me? I thought I knew you, Flint."

"Me? I trusted you, Maggie." He lowered his voice and turned his head to keep what followed more private. "I loved you once. There was a time when I'd have decked the first person who'd suggested you weren't perfect."

"You sure had a funny way of showing it."

"Meaning?"

She heard an approaching vehicle and started across the room to answer the door. "I stayed right here in Serenity, waiting and hoping," she shot back at him. "You knew exactly where to find me."

"You'd turned me down flat," Flint replied. "How was I supposed to know you were in trouble?"

"It wasn't trouble," Maggie said, pausing to smile fondly at her little boy. "It was a blessing in disguise. I didn't realize that for a few months, but eventually it became very, very clear."

The knock was brisk and brief. Maggie opened the door with a smile and stood back. "Thanks for coming, Greg." She gestured. "Wolfie's over there with Mark."

The vet stopped midstride. "And who else?"

"I'd get up and shake your hand," Flint said, "but I'm a little busy here."

Maggie sensed an increase in tension that practically rattled the remaining windows. Greg and Flint were both scowling and facing each other like two rutting bucks. In Flint's case that was probably due to his outdated impression of the veterinarian's stature. Both men had filled out and matured. They were about the same build and while wearing padded jackets seemed equal in strength, although she would have given an edge to Flint in a fight.

"That's Warden Crawford," Maggie said. "Flint, this is Greg. You remember Miss Inez's grandson."

The vet nodded at Flint. "I'd heard you were back in the area."

When Maggie noted Greg's attention flitting between Mark and the warden, she was afraid one of them would say something to make things worse—if that was possible.

"Flint located Wolfie for us and brought him

home," she interjected. "I hope he's not badly hurt."

That lessened the pressure somewhat, particularly when Greg crossed the room, knelt next to the resting dog and began to examine him while Flint eased away.

If the living room had been the size of a football stadium, it would still have felt too small to accommodate the four of them, Maggie realized. The only one who seemed oblivious of the crackling anxiety in the atmosphere was little Mark. All he cared about was seeing that his pet was well cared for.

And all I care about is Mark, Maggie kept insisting. Who was she trying to convince? Herself? Well, she was failing. She cared about her son, yes, but seeing his father's pain and watching him struggle to maintain self-control in the midst of this situation had hit her with a tsunami of emotion, which was now ebbing and flowing like a real tidal wave.

Worst of all, Maggie recalled, Flint had insinuated she might be in cahoots with somebody who wanted to hurt him. She would never even consider causing him purposeful harm because... Because she still loved him.

EIGHT

By the time Flint reached his parked truck, he was at the end of his emotional rope and barely hanging on. It was too much to deal with all at once. Lost years. Lost opportunities. What was he going to do? What *could* he do?

"Take one day at a time," he told himself. "So far, this one has been plenty." The irony of that thought stuck with him long enough to warrant a disgusted chuckle. Myriad questions were whirling through his mind so rapidly that none made much sense.

He didn't have to take a DNA test to prove he was Mark's father. That much was certain. Getting to know the little guy better was going to be a pleasure.

What if Maggie interfered, tried to keep them apart as she had done so far? That notion did not sit well, and he began to realize he'd be wise to get back into her good graces for his own sake, rather than simply to carry out the assignment to locate her kin.

"And stop letting my temper rule my mouth," he added, grimacing. "Accusing her of trying to hurt me was really stupid." In his heart Flint knew better. The old Maggie had been kind and gentle. And in spite of the fact that her newly developed strength of character had them butting heads, deep down he still trusted her.

After loading the ATV in the back of his truck, he slid behind the wheel and waited for the vet to leave. Repeated checks of the time made it seem as if the guy planned to spend the night. That thought tied Flint in a knot. It had been a long time since he'd courted Maggie, and he supposed it was possible that her morals had slipped. He didn't want to think such a thing, but there it was, front and center in his unruly imagination.

What was it the sheriff had said? Maggie had been engaged to several men after he'd left town? Flint's hands gripped the steering wheel so tightly his knuckles turned white. She couldn't have been serious about anyone else, could she? Not when she was already carrying his baby.

His baby. His son. Picturing the innocence and affection in the child's eyes when they'd hugged turned Flint's heart and mind to mush. Was it possible to love a child that quickly?

"Apparently," he murmured, aware of the

strong pull to reenter the house regardless of the lack of welcome he anticipated. "I have to see him again. I have to know more. Maggie owes me at least that much."

Just as Flint was checking the time on his cell phone once more, the front door opened and Greg Gogerty stepped out. Bright light behind Maggie made her seem to glow, and although that threw the vet into shadow, Flint was certain the two shared a brief parting hug.

Unwilling to let their tender moment linger, Flint stepped from his truck and slammed the door to make his presence known.

Greg stepped in front of Maggie, obviously shielding her. "Who is it? Who's out there?"

"Flint Crawford."

"I thought you left." The man's voice radiated animosity.

"Changed my mind," Flint said, approaching the porch as casually as possible. He knew Maggie wouldn't be fooled, but perhaps he could allay the vet's concerns. "I need to have a talk with Ms. Morgan."

Although Greg gave no ground at first, Flint heard Maggie quietly reassure him that she'd be okay before he replied, "If you say so. You have my number. If you need anything else, just give me a call. Night or day."

She smiled. "Thank you. I'll be fine."

I would never have left her alone in a situa-

tion like this, Flint told himself, watching the other man leave. Then again, it was clear that Gogerty had made the familial connection between Flint and Mark, so perhaps that was why he'd given in so easily.

As Flint climbed the porch steps, Maggie's smile faded. Solemn, she stepped away from the doorway, leaving the path open for him to enter.

Without turning she asked, "Coffee?"

"Fine." Flint figured holding a mug would give him something to do with his hands and help keep their conversation from escalating into an argument.

They eased past the dog and boy. Both were sleeping on the throw rug, curled up like two tired pups.

"No other injuries?" Flint asked softly.

"No. Fatigue and blood loss, mostly. Any shards of glass that were stuck in his fur apparently fell out while he was running. It's a good thing he has such a thick coat."

Flint entered the kitchen for the second time that evening, this time taking note of its old-fashioned quaintness. Clearly, the bulk of funds for the sanctuary had been spent on the animal quarters. At least so far. If Ms. Dodd intended to refurbish the house, too, perhaps that was why her niece and nephew thought she was delusional. Doing that job well was going to cost a small fortune.

Instead of sitting, Flint leaned against the edge of the counter, arms crossed, and watched Maggie making coffee. Her hands were shaking, as before, but she was standing tall.

"He seems like a good kid," Flint said.

"Most of the time. All little boys have their moments."

"Not me. I was perfect." He smiled slightly, waiting for her reaction, and was not disappointed. When she whirled to stare at him, Maggie was wide-eyed.

That made him chuckle. "Okay, so maybe not quite perfect, but I did the best I could under the circumstances." He sobered. "I was a handful when Bess and Ira took me in."

"I remember. A lot of girls were fascinated by your bad-boy image."

"Not you?"

Maggie sighed. "I suppose that may have had something to do with the attraction, at first. Once I got to know you I could tell you weren't really such a terrible rebel."

"But I was a Crawford." He grimaced. "The evil product of two generations of unwed women." Realizing what he'd implied, he apologized. "Sorry."

"No need to be sorry. It is what it is. I never once considered getting rid of the baby. He's a gift from God whether his parents were married or not. What happened between you and me is not Mark's fault."

"I know that. Did you think I was blaming him?"

She turned back to the bubbling coffeepot and filled two cups. "I don't know what to think. I suppose you don't, either, or you wouldn't be here now."

Flint followed her to the small kitchen table and sat across from her, waiting until she'd sweetened her coffee before continuing. "I hardly know where to begin. It seems impossible."

Maggie nodded. "It did to me, too. When I began to suspect why I felt funny, my mother took me to the doctor. Even after testing I kept arguing that it had to be a mistake."

"Did your father try to force you to terminate?"

"He probably would have if his health hadn't been so poor." She smiled wistfully. "In a way, Dad's illness helped. He passed away before Mark was born and Mom was there for me, even though she's a Witherspoon."

"You do see the idiocy of that old feud, don't you?"

"Of course I do." Her voice was raised. "But apparently you don't."

"What's that supposed to mean?"

"Well, you did leave town."

"Only after you refused to marry me."

Maggie pushed away from the table and jumped to her feet. "I did nothing of the kind."

"You refused to come away with me."

She was rolling her eyes. "Oh, please. I didn't want to elope, that's all. How was I supposed to know you'd up and take off the way you did?"

"Because I told you so."

"Ha! You did nothing of the kind. I sat there in my prom dress for hours, waiting for you, and you never came."

Puzzled, Flint wondered how their communication had gotten so mixed up. He was positive he'd not only discussed his plans for joining the military, but he'd also sent Maggie a good-bye note.

"I can see we're not going to get our past ironed out in one sitting, so let's talk about the future."

The look she sent him reminded him of a doe pinned by the headlights of a speeding car, unable to flee to save herself. When she said, "What future?" he knew he had his work cut out for him.

"Mark's future," Flint said. "You know who he looks like as well as I do, so you may as well admit it." He scowled at her.

"No way. Leave me alone."

"Not until you and I figure out how to protect our son."

"I'm doing just fine, thank you. Mark is a happy, healthy child."

"With parents who have both been shot at and a mother who was run off the road and chased through the forest. What if he'd been with you that night?"

"He wasn't."

"Not then. What about the next time?"

"I can take care of my family."

"*Our* family," Flint insisted. "Mark is my son, too."

"Get out!" Maggie ordered.

Calm on the outside, stomach roiling, Flint faced her. "If you make me take you to court and sue for my parental rights, I will."

"I said, get out." She pointed with her whole arm. "We have nothing more to talk about."

"Yes, we do. Think, Maggie. You love the boy. I know you do. So let's work together to keep him safe." If that sensible suggestion didn't get through to her, he didn't know what would.

"There was no trouble around here until you showed up again," Maggie insisted with a raised voice. "Whatever is wrong, you're the cause."

He reached for her hand, tried to grasp it, but she yanked away. "Think," he said. "We're both victims and stuck between two warring sides. You and I didn't cause the feud. We want nothing to do with it. But we're still in somebody's crosshairs. Until we get to the bottom of the problem, nobody is safe, especially not Mark."

"Leave him out of this. He's my responsibility and I'll send him away if I see fit. You have no say in the matter."

"It wasn't enough to hide him from me for five years?"

The contrition Flint had expected to see did not appear. Instead, Maggie flung open the back door and shouted, "I would have been delighted if you'd never met him. My father was right. You're trouble with a capital *T.* I want you out of my life."

Flint knew lingering was useless. Once tempers flared, logic went out the window. If Maggie wouldn't plan with him, he'd take steps to guard his son on his own. True, the boy wasn't up to his neck in the feud—yet. But let one of the old-timers like Elwood decide Mark was a true Crawford and everything could change.

In the blink of an eye.

Maggie was so angry she wanted to throw her coffee cup across the room, preferably at Flint's head. Fortunately, he was through the door before she could decide to act.

"This is *exactly* what I was afraid of," she grumbled.

A small voice answered, "What's wrong, Mama?"

And this, Maggie added silently, bending to

kiss the top of Mark's head and ruffle his hair. "Nothing's wrong. I'm sorry if I woke you." She glanced past him. "How's Wolfie? Is he leaving his bandage alone this time?"

"Uh-huh." Mark peered into the kitchen. "Where did the man go?"

"You mean the veterinarian?"

"No. The nice one. The one who found Wolfie and brought him back."

"You were awake when the warden left, honey. Remember?"

Mark shook his head. "Uh-uh. He came back. I saw him. I was hoping he'd like me and stay."

"Everybody likes you. You know that."

"Yeah." He scuffed the toe of his slipper on the floor. "'Cept Johnny and Kyle. They said I was a ba—"

Maggie clamped her hand over the child's mouth before he could finish. "Don't ever say that again. Understand? You're just as good as they are. God made you special and He doesn't make mistakes."

"Then why did Wolfie get hurt?"

The first answer that came to Maggie involved Flint, so she rejected it. "Sometimes we do things we shouldn't and we get hurt. That's all."

"Like what?"

His little face was upturned, his expression one of abject trust. Maggie yearned to confide in him, and would have, if he'd been a few years older. Someday the whole truth would be clear to Mark and he could then decide if he wanted to connect with his father. But in the meantime, Flint Crawford was *not* going to get his hands on her baby. Not as long as there was breath in her body.

Which reminded her of the recent close calls Flint had cited. Okay, maybe he did have a point. She could see wisdom in breaking up her routine and being less predictable, not to mention letting her son spend more time at Faye's. While Mark was in town with his granny, he was also much closer to the police station and among friends, rather than being isolated out at the compound with her.

Tomorrow she'd see what her mother thought of having a temporary houseguest. Given the way Faye loved the little boy, Maggie knew there would be no problem leaving them together a bit more. And she'd worry about Mark a lot less if he was in a familiar place than if she allowed Flint to interfere.

It didn't matter what his so-called plans were. She wanted nothing to do with them.

"It's past your bedtime, Mark, honey. You need to go to sleep."

"Can I sleep with Wolfie some more?"

Maggie smiled at the sweet remembrance. "How about if I take him to your room and help him up on the bed with you? That way you'll know if he's being a good boy and leaving his bandages alone."

"Wolfie can sleep with me? Yeah!"

"Only for a few nights. Just until he gets better and it's safe to let him walk around by himself. Dr. Greg said we should be able to take off the bandage soon."

Grinning at his youthful enthusiasm, she followed him to where the dog was dozing. Medication had left the enormous canine in somewhat of a stupor, but he managed to rouse himself enough to stand, with Maggie's help.

She encircled the massive chest and lifted to keep weight off his sore paw. His rear end hobbled along, Mark pretending to support his bushy tail. "I'm helping."

"I can see that." Maggie would have doubled up laughing if she hadn't been straining to transport a half-limp dog bigger than a German shepherd and hairier than Sasquatch.

She heaved Wolfie's front end onto the coverlet on Mark's bed, then quickly grabbed his waist to lift the rear. To her relief he stayed where she put him, panting and already starting to close his eyes again.

"Okay, Mark. You have my permission to move your pillow and cuddle up with him if you want. I'll get an extra quilt and cover both of you."

"Thank you, Mama," he said sweetly, already

curled up beside his best pal and patting the massive rib cage.

As Maggie laid more covers over them both and smiled tenderly, she wondered if she'd ever seen a more charming picture of pure love.

The easy answer sobered her. "Yes," she whispered, looking for words to describe the images of Mark abruptly hugging Flint and the man's compassionate response.

Only then, as she replayed the scene, did she realize that when Flint had pressed his face to the child's shoulder, there were unshed tears glistening in his emerald eyes.

She'd been so worried about Mark's possible rejection she hadn't paid much attention to other details and wondered if she was imagining raw emotions because hers were in such a state.

Padding off to bed, Maggie let her mind replay the evening in its entirety. If she'd kept a diary, there wouldn't have been enough blank pages to list every fact, let alone mention how she'd felt as the scene unfolded.

Thankfully, that trial was over. For now. And although she was still anxious about the future, she figured she was weary enough to go to sleep despite her concerns.

The house was dark except for the bluish glow of a tiny night-light in the bathroom. Sighing, she closed her eyes and snuggled into her pillow.

The next thing Maggie knew, something woke

her. A sound? She'd been dreaming so vividly she wasn't sure. Had there been a faint squeak of hinges?

She sat up in bed. All the unexpected company had disrupted her usual nighttime schedule. She knew she'd snapped the dead bolt on the kitchen door after Flint left, but what about the front? Picturing Flint entering for the second time, she failed to see herself passing him in order to secure that lock.

Eyes wide and trying to adjust to the lack of light, Maggie held her breath. The house was as silent as an old structure ever was. Changes in temperature and humidity made the boards groan and sometimes make popping noises, but that was normal.

The blue glow from the hallway remained steady. Undisturbed. Nevertheless, she had a strong urge to check on her "boys." All she had to do was gather enough courage to leave the sanctuary of her own room. A strong maternal instinct made that easier. Being unarmed was the only aspect that gave her pause.

She swung her legs over the side of the bed and put on a robe and slippers while she cast around for some kind of weapon. The only solid object nearby was a small bedside lamp. Pulling the plug, she gripped it like a baseball bat and started down the hall.

A shadow flickered. Or did it? Maggie froze.

Braced herself. Waited for what seemed like an eternity.

Nothing more happened. There were no strange sounds, no changes in the night-light's glow.

Feeling a bit silly, she began to relax. The lamp held lower, she proceeded to tiptoe toward Mark's room.

Just as she reached the doorway, she heard Wolfie growl. Assuming he was reacting to her stealthy approach, Maggie spoke soothingly. "It's okay, boy. It's just me."

His barking erupted as if he'd just spotted an archenemy. Startled, Maggie was about to re-assure him again when she was unexpectedly shoved aside. All she saw was the blurred pas-sage of a dark figure.

The lamp hit the floor. Its bulb shattered. Act-ing on instinct, she pivoted into the boy's bed-room, slammed the door shut and jammed her shoulder against it to keep it closed.

Maggie slid to the floor, her back pressing against the door.

As she opened her arms to embrace her two frightened companions, she realized that, like it or not, Flint had been right. She could not pro-tect Mark adequately by herself.

NINE

Maggie's heartbeats thudded in her ears. They were safe for the moment. At least she hoped so. Wolfie was panting and licking tears from Mark's face while the child clung to her and sobbed with fright.

They needed help. Reinforcements. The police. But how was she going to notify anybody when her phone was outside this room? What might happen if she dared open the door to go fetch it?

Just then the thin glass of the broken light-bulb crunched. Someone was walking across it! Maggie didn't dream she could get more tense, but she did.

After that, however, there was nothing else audible. No steps, no pounding knock, no voiced threats.

Straining to listen, she prayed she'd hear something more definitive. Something that would tell her that the prowler had fled—an engine, fading footsteps, anything.

Darkness enfolded her, pressing in to smother. Long minutes passed with no sign that their enemy still lurked.

"That doesn't mean he's gone," Maggie muttered. She gently unwound Mark's arms from her neck and pulled him into her lap, where she stroked his silky hair.

Her pulse was starting to slow. Words of comfort were getting easier. "It's okay, honey. Whoever scared us isn't making noise anymore."

She felt his nod against her shoulder. "I need to get my phone so I can call the sheriff."

Mark gripped her again. "No!"

"It'll be okay. I promise." Maggie studied the familiar room and made a strategic decision. "Tell you what. While I'm gone, you and Wolfie can make a special camp in the closet, just the two of you."

"I wanna stay with you."

"I know you do." Maggie managed to swallow past the lump of emotion in her throat. It was crazy to bide her time and wait for the prowler to return, perhaps with reinforcements, yet did it make any more sense to venture out when he might be hiding in wait for her? Neither choice made much sense. She figured she could either muster her courage, hope no one was waiting to ambush her and go for the cell phone, or sit there helpless all night. Action seemed the most logical course.

"Where's the little flashlight I gave you?" she asked her son.

"Over there."

"See if you can find it and take it with you in case you need it in your new camp."

"Okay." He left and returned in moments.

Maggie covered the beam with her fingers as she tested the light. In the glow that escaped she could see Mark's worried expression. Moreover, they both noticed that Wolfie's paw was bleeding through his bandage.

"Mama, look!"

"I see it, honey. Don't worry about that now. It's not bad enough to hurt him," Maggie said, forcing herself to mimic being calm when she wanted to shriek.

She grabbed a blanket off the bed and tossed it on the floor for their temporary comfort. "There you go. Into the closet with you both."

As soon as they were settled with Mark hugging the big dog's neck, she held out the flashlight. "Here. Just don't turn it on unless you really have to. We don't want anybody to see the light and figure out where you are."

"You said the bad guy was gone." Mark's voice was reedy, quavering.

"I'm just being very careful, that's all. Promise you'll stay right there with Wolfie?"

He nodded. "I promise."

"Okay." Easing the closet door shut, Maggie whispered, "I love you."

"I love you, too, Mama."

She closed her eyes long enough to add, "Please, God, keep him safe," then started for the hall.

Once again the blue glow illuminated her path. She paused to listen, to muster the necessary bravery to proceed. From now on she was going to sleep with her cell phone, even if she had to sew a zippered pocket onto her pajamas.

Hands fisted, she skirted the broken glass and pieces of ceramic lamp base. Each step after that came faster until she was running. She dove for her purse, carried it across her rumpled bed with her and began a frantic search in its depths.

The moment her hand tightened on the cell phone she felt some relief, but that was nothing compared to how glad she was when the 911 operator answered.

As far as Flint was concerned, his conversations with Maggie had only just begun. Yes, he was angry. But more than that he was disappointed. And extremely worried.

It had occurred to him that his return to Serenity might have been the catalyst for the trouble she'd been having—that they'd both been having, counting the wild shots he'd dodged. If his own safety had been the only consideration, he'd have been okay with it. Lots of folks weren't fans of Game and Fish wardens. Or of laws. He'd been threatened before.

But everything had changed the moment Flint saw Mark. Everything. It really didn't matter what he did at this point, because it was too late to turn back the clock. Not only was it clear to plenty of people how much he and the boy looked alike, but it was clear to *him.* There was no returning to the bliss of ignorance. His and Maggie's genes had created a wondrous child. Their child. And whether she liked it or not, he intended to look out for both mother and son.

What Flint would have loved to do was confide in his great-grandparents the way he used to as a teenager. Sadly, Ira was likely to erupt in senseless anger and Bess would support whatever her husband wanted. Right now the old couple needed his help around the farm, and the fewer waves he made in their established routines, the better it would be for all concerned.

That left a buddy from the service whose number was still packed away with his discharge papers, or the town sheriff. Harlan had made him feel more welcome than anyone else. Flint checked the time. It was far too late to phone, but maybe a text would be okay.

All he typed was R U up? Not expecting any answer until morning, he put his cell aside and lay back in bed. When it beeped a minute later he jumped to grab it.

Why? Harlan had texted.

Need to talk.

About?

Flint hesitated, then spelled Maggie and waited for a typed reply. Instead, his phone rang. It was the sheriff.

"How did you find out?" Harlan asked without saying hello.

Flint gripped the instrument tighter, his heartbeats picking up speed. "Find out what?"

"She thought she had a prowler tonight. The kid said he saw a moving shadow, but I didn't find any sign of a break in."

"But she's okay?"

"Yes. She's sure that dog of hers messed up his foot again chasin' some guy off. Other than that, everything's under control."

"Are you still out at her place?" Flint asked, trying to dress one-handed.

"Sittin' in her driveway. Just about to call it quits unless there's more trouble. You plannin' on comin' over?"

"Yes. Wait for me?"

"Sure, son. The night's shot anyway. Might as well stay up for breakfast."

The only parts of his regular uniform Flint donned were his boots. And his gun.

Once Harlan had pronounced Maggie's home prowler free and she'd rechecked all the locks the way she usually did before retiring, she cleaned up the mess and settled herself in Mark's room. She'd have preferred to bring in the firewood chopping ax for their protection, but given the danger of the sharp blade, she'd opted for a hoe with a strong handle instead.

"I'm not sleepy," Mark whined.

"Me, either. We need to hold still just the same so Wolfie doesn't jump around on his sore foot."

"Is it bleedin' again?" He rolled over and bounced on his knees on the mattress.

"It will be if you keep that up," Maggie warned. "We need to be very nice to him for scaring that bad guy away."

"Yeah. He was real ugly," Mark offered.

That took Maggie aback. "You saw his face?"

The boy shrugged, then threw himself onto his back with a whoosh. "Kinda."

"Why didn't you tell me before?"

"I dunno."

"Mark…" She drew out his name. "If you know something that I don't, you need to tell me. It's important. The sheriff needs to know stuff like that."

"'Cause he has a badge?"

"That's right." Maggie kept monitoring the dog's paw, thankful to see no more seepage.

"The game warden has a badge, too."

"Yes, he does." She was beginning to see where the clever boy was going with his questions. "But it's the sheriff who checks on people. Game wardens look after animals."

"People, too. I heard you tell Mamaw."

Maggie sighed in resignation. "You weren't supposed to be listening."

"Why not?"

"Because it was grown-up talk."

"What's the difference?" he asked with an impish grin.

Maggie had to chuckle. "Good question. How about from now on I tell you when you're not supposed to be listening? Will that help?"

"Sure," he said. The twinkle in his Crawford-green eyes said otherwise.

Laughing softly, Maggie tucked covers around her son and herself, taking care to include as much of the dog as possible while leaving his cut paw sticking out. As soon as they both settled down she'd go outside and bring Harlan up to speed about the prowler being "ugly." If he'd left by then she'd phone him in the morning. Being ugly was hardly a useful description.

After about ten minutes she heard a motor and saw twin beams of light sweep across the bedroom ceiling. If the car had been the sheriff, leaving, his headlights would not have hit the house.

"Rats. More company," she whispered, hoping Mark was too drowsy to pay attention. Apparently, he and the dog both were, because neither of them stirred when she slid from beneath their shared blankets.

One peek through her front windows told her that not only was the sheriff's patrol car still there, but a silver state truck was now parked beside it, nose to tail, so the drivers could easily converse.

Maggie wasn't positive that Harlan had called Flint, but she had her suspicions. If it turned out that he was keeping the warden informed about her, she intended to raise the roof. There was no reason for Game and Fish to be notified if the Dodd Sanctuary was not directly involved. No reason at all. At least nothing valid.

She stormed into her room and pulled on jeans and a sweatshirt before stuffing her feet into boots. It was time to put a stop to this good-old-boy network nonsense. She certainly didn't want to have to avoid reporting a crime just to keep Flint's nose out of her personal life.

By the time she was dressed, she'd decided that angry confrontation was not the best approach. Instead, she went into the kitchen to make coffee. Enough for three.

Then Maggie put on her jacket, finger-combed her hair and headed for the confab in the driveway. No way was she going to let Flint and the sheriff get away with keeping her in the dark. Whatever was going on was just as much her problem as theirs.

Her breath hitched as she quietly eased the front door closed behind her. It was *more* her problem. She had Mark's future to worry about. God willing, she'd make it through these current attacks and live to see him grow to adulthood.

And if not? she asked herself, realizing it was a justifiable question. "If something happens to me, Father," she prayed, "please take care of my son."

Had God already answered that plea by bringing his father into the picture? Maggie wondered.

She stood tall, gathered her courage and started down the porch steps.

Harlan leaned out his car window and gestured with his chin. "Heads up. Trouble's on the way."

"So I see. I'm kind of surprised she'd come out after you said she was so scared earlier."

"Nothing about Miz Maggie Morgan surprises me," the sheriff said. "She's quite a gal."

Flint didn't know how to respond without sounding infatuated, so he just nodded.

"Think about it. There she is, a pregnant teen-ager with nobody to love her, a dying daddy, a flaky mother and an uncle with a police record as long as your arm. Did she run? Or hide? Nope. She got herself a job and worked as long as she could, then moved in with her widowed mama in order to survive while she took college courses by computer."

"I didn't know that," Flint said. He was watching her approach in the side mirror of his truck.

"There's probably a lot you don't know," Harlan huffed. "But I get the idea you're about to learn more."

"Yeah. I'll pull forward and park. You're staying, aren't you?"

That made the older man chuckle. "Why? You ain't scared of a little thing like Maggie, are you?"

Flint grinned back at him. "Terrified."

At first, it upset Maggie to think Flint was leaving. When he parked and got out, however, she didn't know whether or not to be glad.

"I put on a big pot of fresh coffee," she called, careful to include the sheriff. "Why don't we go inside and drink it instead of you guys sitting out here in your cars?" She chaffed her palms. "It's freezing."

"Predictions of snow for next week," Harlan

said, ambling over to join her. "Got any pancakes to go with that coffee?"

"I might be able to scare some up." Maggie smiled at him, then diverted her gaze to Flint and quipped, "Even if you bring him."

The lighthearted diversion apparently worked, because Flint's shoulders began to relax and his walk seemed less awkward. Would they ever regain the easy camaraderie they had once shared? She doubted it.

Maggie paused at the front door, briefly blocking the way. "Shush. The boys are asleep and I'd like them to stay that way."

Both men nodded. In the glow from the porch light, the green of Flint's eyes looked exactly like Mark's. The more she saw of this man, the more she associated him with their son. Part of her problem was undoubtedly that she loved her little boy so totally. The difficulty came when her heart and mind applied those same emotions to Flint.

The kitchen was welcomingly warm. Maggie shed her jacket and left the men to find themselves comfortable seats at the table while she filled three mugs and delivered them.

Sighing, she smiled at Harlan. "One cup of coffee first and then I'll start your pancakes, Sheriff. I just need to wake myself up a little more."

Out of the corner of her eye, she saw Flint

wrap both hands around his mug and lean forward, elbows and forearms resting on the table. "What happened tonight?"

"I'm sure Harlan has already told you," she replied, making a face. "I probably couldn't sneeze without you showing up to hand me a hanky."

"That's because I care, Maggie. We both do."

Flint hadn't moved, yet seemed closer somehow. She nodded. "I'm getting that idea."

A snort of amusement from the older man didn't help Maggie's mood. When she tried to glare at him and saw his comical expression, she found herself snickering instead.

"All right, all right." She took a sip of coffee and leaned back in her chair to claim a little distance. "The sheriff has the mistaken idea I may have imagined it, but I know I didn't. Wolfie went nuts and Mark said he saw somebody, too."

"Did he recognize the prowler?"

She made a face at Flint before replying, "No. But he did tell me later that the guy was ugly. Wolfie charged at him, sounding like he was about to eat him for supper, and the man knocked me down in his rush to get away. That's what made the dog's paw start bleeding again."

Tension radiated from the game warden. "You think this prowler was after the boy?"

"I don't know. If he didn't know the layout of the house, he might have just been exploring." It had already occurred to her that Abigail's niece and nephew had probably visited as children, if not as adults, and she had to quell a shiver. "As soon as Wolfie alerted, somebody in a black hoodie pushed past me and hightailed it."

"How did he get in?"

She slid lower in her chair. "That was my fault. After you went out the back door, I was so…distracted…I guess I forgot to lock the front again."

"You don't have a regular routine? Unbelievable."

"Don't raise your voice to me, Flint Crawford. Of course I have a routine. I always go around and check all the doors and windows before I go to bed."

"But not this time."

"No. Not this time."

"Harlan said a lamp was broken." He glanced at the sheriff. "Right? If the guy touched it, there might be prints."

The older man huffed. "Nope. That was Maggie's weapon. She's the one who dropped it."

Flint rounded on her. "A lamp? That's almost as useless as a rotten limb."

Judging by the firm set of his jaw and glint in his eyes, Flint was growing angrier by the minute. "Serves me right for telling you anything," she countered. "Be sure to put plenty of syrup on your pancakes, Warden Crawford. You need a lot of sweetening."

"And you need to learn to shoot," he called after her.

Maggie whirled. "I help injured creatures, I don't harm them. I don't even like to step on bugs—and this is Arkansas, so there are plenty of those. Why would I want to shoot a gun?"

"Self-defense, if nothing else. You're out here in the middle of nowhere with no protection."

"He's got a point there," the sheriff said. "Until we figure out why all these crazy things have been happening to you, it makes sense to take precautions."

"I trust God. That's all I need." Maggie turned her back to them.

Flint wasn't about to back down. "Oh, really?"

Maggie could tell he was coming closer, because his aura preceded him. Tiny hairs on her arms prickled and a shiver zinged up her spine.

"Do you trust God or are you tempting Him?" Flint asked. "He gave you brains. You're supposed to use them to figure things out, such as who might have been prowling around in your house."

Spinning around again, she found him standing directly behind her, so close they were almost touching. That was so unnerving, she spoke before thinking. "If I'd used my brains in the past, I'd have listened to my parents and stayed away from you."

Hostility that had been sparking between them

suddenly vanished like smoke. She saw a flash of pain that he failed to hide quickly enough. The green eyes began to glisten and their emotional reaction reached all the way to Maggie's tender heart.

She touched his arm. "I'm sorry. I shouldn't have said that."

"Yes, you should. You're right. We were wrong for each other in so many ways. But we were young and foolish. We thought we were in love."

We were, she countered silently, unwilling to break eye contact or step away.

"I'm sorry for all you had to go through," Flint whispered, bending even closer.

Their lips were mere inches apart. Was he going to kiss her? Did she want him to? What should she do if he did? With the sheriff in the room, there was no chance Flint would assume she was going to swoon and fall into his arms, so it was probably okay to accept one kiss. Just one, though. For old times' sake and to heal the distress she'd just caused him. It had not been her intention to hurt his feelings. If there had been a way to snatch back her caustic comment about their failed relationship, she would have.

Her eyelashes fluttered. Her lids lowered partway. Maggie held her breath and waited.

The moment passed. Flint strode to the table and picked up the mugs, behaving as if nothing special had happened between them. "Okay. So far we know the prowler was ugly. That fits half the guys in Serenity, if you ask me. Any other ideas, Sheriff?"

"I still have my officers looking for clues along the highway where Maggie wrecked, and you put your guys on the wolf ruse, right?"

"Right. Looks like that's a dead end. Nobody found signs of a pack of wolves in the area." He lifted the coffeepot. "Refill anybody?"

If Maggie hadn't had the kitchen counter to lean against, she might have staggered. Her equilibrium was certainly upset. And her pride was in shambles. When she should be celebrating a narrow escape from Flint's unwanted advances, she was actually so disappointed she could have wept.

She grabbed a whisk and took her frustrations out on the pancake batter. Those were the lightest, fluffiest hotcakes she'd ever made.

TEN

By the time Flint had endured breakfast at Maggie's, he was ready for one of Ira's daily naps. Instead, his assignment took him up on Nine Mile Ridge to check a report of white-tail deer poachers who had left behind everything from the animals except tenderloin. It was disgusting. He was still muttering about wasteful gluttons when he got back to regional headquarters in Mammoth Spring to handle the pile of paperwork that had accumulated. Clearly, he had been spending too much time in Serenity.

Wardens Samson and Wallace both looked up when he entered, greeted him, then found reasons to immediately head for the break room. As Samson passed he cocked his head toward the private office of Captain Lang. That was not a good sign. Neither was the sight of Lang standing in his doorway, beckoning.

Flint hitched his duty belt and stood tall. He hadn't worked out of this office long enough to know the captain well, but it was pretty clear that the man had something serious to say.

"Yes, sir?"

Lang closed his office door. "Have a seat."

Flint assumed he was about to receive a reprimand and was surprised when his superior didn't launch into a tirade.

"How are you coming with the Morgan woman? Have you asked her how we can locate Witherspoon?"

"I did bring it up. She wasn't cooperative in the least and I haven't managed to pin her down since."

"Well, work through your problems with her and get us some answers. I took a chance sending you over there without backup because I thought I could trust you. Don't disappoint me."

"I won't," Flint promised. "He's a recluse. Without specific information we might never run across him. He knows that backcountry better than anybody."

Leaning back in his desk chair, Lang appeared to be mulling over a decision. When he said, "I'll give you one more week. Finish this," Flint's heart sank.

"Do whatever it takes. I want to close Elwood's file for good."

"There's something you should know," Flint explained. "Maggie and I have both suffered unprovoked attacks since I came back." He pointed to a stack of forms in the captain's in-box. "I reported shots being fired at me several times. And Maggie was run off the road and her place was broken into."

"What makes you think there's a connection?"

This was the first test, Flint realized, his chance to own up to his past mistakes. "Because she and I have a connection. We have a son."

"Whoa." Lang's eyebrows rose. "That's not in your personnel file."

"I just found out," Flint said with a deep sigh.

"Talk about complications."

"Yeah." Flint rose and began to pace the small office. "And that's not all. There's also an old feud between the Crawfords and the Witherspoons to consider. That's one of the reasons it never worked out between Maggie and me. Our extended families hated each other. As far as I know, though, the only old-timer who is still likely to stir up trouble is Elwood. Maybe if I can prove enough to land him in jail for poaching it'll solve both our problems."

Lang steepled his fingers. "I can always put Samson or Wallace on it instead."

"That won't help. There's no way I can stop being involved," Flint said flatly. "Even if I transferred out tomorrow, Maggie might still be in danger, not to mention our little boy, Mark."

Nodding, the captain said, "All right. We'll work with what we have. What's your plan?"

If the situation hadn't been so dire, Flint might have laughed. "Plan? So far I've been a step behind whoever is harassing us since this whole thing started."

"You've brought in local police?"

"Yes. Right away. Maggie lives in the county and the sheriff has been a lot of help."

"How about city or state police?"

"I'd rather not involve too many more departments until I get a better handle on the situation," Flint said. "Some of the suspects are good old boys with hunting in their blood. They know every inch of the woods around Serenity. I'd hate to feel responsible for getting some street cop hurt just because he's used to paved roads and sidewalks."

"*Some* of the suspects? Who else?"

"There are a couple of people who have a financial ax to grind regarding the Dodd Sanctuary. They made actual threats against Ms. Morgan."

"Okay. Keep me posted." He gestured at the overflowing in-box. "If anything else happens, report directly to me."

"Yes, sir."

"Just don't blow it." Lang was scowling. "I'm nearing retirement age and I don't want to lose my pension over you and your girlfriend."

Flint opened his mouth to insist that Maggie wasn't his girlfriend, then changed his mind.

Whether she was or not, she was still in some-one's crosshairs. That was all that mattered. That, and keeping her and Mark safe.

Nothing critical lay beyond those goals.

The next couple of days passed in a blur for Maggie. She went through the motions of car-ing for her animals and getting her son to and from school safely, but she could not seem to relax. Mostly, she kept waiting for the next di-saster to occur.

When she spotted someone in dirty camo working his way through the woods behind her compound, she figured he was bringing trouble. By the time she recognized her fifteen-year-old cousin, Robbie, she was so tense she was ready to make a dash for the house.

He casually raised an arm. Relieved, Mag-gie waved back and called, "Hi. You looking for work? I could use more firewood split."

The youth shrugged. "Sure. I guess."

"What's wrong, Robbie?"

He scuffed the toe of his worn boot through loose leaves. "Nothin'. Just heading for town."

"Do you need a ride?"

"Naw. Luke and Will are picking me up down by your mailbox in a little bit."

Maggie was relieved the others would be stop-ping half a mile away. She trusted her youngest cousin, but the two older ones were too much like their grandfather. They reveled in causing mayhem and laughed while they watched others suffer. She'd seen them do it more than once.

Which reminded her... "Hey, Robbie, I've got a question for you."

"Sure."

"Do you know anything about the truck that ran me off the road last week?"

His shocked expression answered before he spoke. "What truck?"

"That's what I was asking you. I was on my way to town and ended up in a ditch out by Anderson's place."

The tall, thin young man tugged his baseball cap lower over his forehead and shook his head. "Nope. First I've heard of it. Glad you're okay."

"Thanks." She paused, giving herself time to choose her next words very carefully. "How about the shootings?"

This time, he averted his gaze. "Don't know nothin' about no shooting. I been trappin'."

"All right. I just thought maybe Elwood had been messin' with me. Trying to scare me."

"Why would he do that?"

"Because Flint Crawford is back," Maggie told him, watching for signs that he already knew—and there they were. Robbie twitched and dropped his head forward to hide his face behind the bill of his cap while he kicked at more dry leaves.

"Here's what I want you to do for me, Robbie," she said. "Tell Uncle Elwood to leave me alone. Your brothers, too. I haven't bothered any of you and I expect the same courtesy. All I'm trying to do here is help injured animals. Just because I happen to know a game warden does not make me your enemy. Got that?"

"Yes, ma'am." He cast a furtive glance down at the dirt road. "I better get going. Luke's driving and he won't wait if I'm late."

"What kind of truck has he got now?" Maggie didn't figure the kid was naive enough to reveal anything criminal, but she had to try.

"A new Dodge." Robbie finally smiled. "It's a real sweet ride."

"Is Will jealous?"

"Naw. He's got him a three-quarter-ton Ford."

"I suppose Elwood's still driving that rusty old International?"

She saw Robbie stiffen. "Why?"

"Because the guy who ran me off the road was driving a dark-colored truck."

"Ha! Then you can forget blamin' my papaw. His truck is the same color it always was. Red."

Maggie forced a smile. Between the oxidation of the paint and rust on the frame, it was still possible that her adversary had been Elwood.

She pictured the attack truck, idling on the shoulder of the highway. Robbie was right! That vehicle couldn't have belonged to Elwood. If it had, she'd have noticed a lot more overall deterioration and less fresh damage.

"I apologize, Robbie," she said. "You're right. The truck that sideswiped me couldn't have been the International. For one thing, the style was newer, more streamlined."

Seeing his body language improve, she added, "Remember. Any time you want to come back and split me a rick or two of firewood, just do it and I'll pay you. Same as last year."

He smiled. "I'm a lot bigger than I used to be. Shouldn't take me near as long."

"It's the finished product that matters," Maggie assured him. "If predictions are right, we're going to have a rough winter."

"Yes, ma'am. I'll do it right soon."

"Is your papaw fixed for winter? The old cabin he favors leaks like a sieve."

"Oh, he ain't livin' there no more. He's got a place…" The teenager broke off with a stricken expression. "Gotta go."

Watching him jog away down her unpaved driveway, Maggie pondered the unexpected modifications of her suspicions. As far as she was concerned, Luke and Will were suspects in the shootings because of their family ties to Elwood, but if they had been the attackers on the highway, they'd have had to borrow a different truck. She found that highly unlikely.

Of course, if she discounted the old feud, the

wild shots could have come from anybody who happened to dislike game wardens. There were plenty of those folks around, ready to take a potshot any time they got the opportunity. Part of that attitude arose from a survival mind-set. There had been a time in the last century when the only way a man could feed his family was to hunt. In or out of season, deer, rabbits and even squirrels meant the difference between life and death. There was always somebody out hunting, legal or not. The only oddity was that other wardens hadn't reported similar attacks recently.

Maggie shivered. The difference between life and death for her and her son might also be hanging in the balance. How could she protect Mark when she couldn't put a face to her enemies? *Yes, plural.* The way she saw it, there had to be more than one person involved. And whoever was behind the unwarranted attacks was either a very bad shot or a very good one. She almost wished it was the latter. At least that way there would be less chance of accidentally being wounded.

Of course, that also meant the marksman could drop her in a heartbeat from the length of a football field.

She pulled her cell from her pocket and thumbed Faye's number. "Hi, Mom. I need another favor."

"As long as it includes my grandson, you have it."

"Matter of fact, it does. Since it's Friday, could you get Mark from school like you have been and keep him over the weekend?" She wanted to say *indefinitely* but thought better of it. One, she didn't want to be separated from her little boy. And two, she didn't want to frighten Faye. At present, it was enough to simply leave Mark with his grandma and go about her business at the sanctuary. If push came to shove she'd explain. Hopefully, it wouldn't be necessary.

"My pleasure," Faye said. "We're still on for Sunday dinner after church, aren't we?"

Maggie's only uncertainty came from wanting to protect her loved ones. "Well, if I can work it out."

"What's to work out? You can meet me and Mark at church and we'll all go out together, same as always."

"How about a pizza this time?" Maggie knew she should break out of her normal rut as much as possible. "You go on home with Mark and I'll stop to pick one up. We can eat at your house."

Faye laughed lightly. "You aren't fooling me, young lady. You just want to come over here to eat so you can lug that domesticated wolf along."

"You've got me figured out," Maggie replied. "But Wolfie really is a dog. I promise."

"If you say so. I'm working in the church nursery this week. I'll put Mark in his class before I start and you can get him after the service."

"Um, no," Maggie said, wondering how much she was eventually going to have to reveal. "I'd rather he stayed with one of us. That's okay, isn't it?"

"Sure, but—"

"I'll explain everything over pizza."

"You'd better. What about Saturday? Are you coming by at all?"

"That depends," Maggie said.

"On what?"

"A lot of things." Like whether or not she saw Flint and had a chance to talk him into accompanying her to the church they had once attended as a loving couple. She had persevered, repented and renewed her faith there years ago, but Flint had not. If he did go with her again, she wasn't sure what kind of reception he'd get. Most members of the congregation were loving and forgiving, but they also thought of her as family, meaning they might stand against him if they thought he was going to hurt her again.

Her mind was so filled with memories she barely heard her mother bid her goodbye. Truth to tell, it didn't matter if she and Flint rekindled their friendship as long as one of them was able to keep Mark safe from harm.

Even if it isn't me? Yes, she answered honestly. Flint would be a good father to the little boy. She'd known that the moment she saw them together. And she was ashamed of her initial jealousy. If her true concern was for Mark's welfare, it shouldn't matter who eventually raised him to adulthood.

Tears filled Maggie's eyes. It shouldn't. But it did. She desperately wanted to live a long and productive life. Who wouldn't? Sometimes it seemed really unfair when mean old codgers like Elwood and Ira reached a ripe old age while younger folks passed away. Then again, terrible sadness could bring eventual joy and acceptance the way her pregnancy had. What had seemed the worst event in her life had turned out to be the biggest blessing, meaning she should learn to trust God and rely more on Jesus, as her pastor often preached.

Shivering over lingering thoughts of her great-uncle and cousins she cast a furtive glance at the silent forest. Dried leaves were floating down. A few birds called. Sunlight reached the ground in wide swaths now that the trees were nearly bare. This should be a peaceful place, a refuge for her as well as the wild animals in the compound. And it had been until Missy and her brother had tried to put a legal end to Abigail's sponsorship.

Or until Flint had shown up. There was no getting around the connection. Maggie didn't think for a second that he had purposely caused the upheavals in her life, but she did blame him for returning and complicating everything.

Maggie shook her head and muttered in disgust. For years she had pleaded with God to bring back the man she loved. Now that He had done that, here she stood, arguing that it had been a mistake. She couldn't have it both ways.

A sense of unrest tickled the hairs at the nape of her neck. She stiffened. Listened. Nothing seemed to have changed, yet it had. Subtly.

Instinct pushed her to quickly complete her chores and retreat to the house. She might be brave, but she wasn't foolhardy enough to putter around outside when the next bullet might snuff out her life.

Every heartbeat, every breath, was a divine gift. She was not going to knowingly risk losing one moment the Lord had given her.

She just wished life came with easy instructions because right now she was about as confused as a person could get.

ELEVEN

Wardens Samson and Wallace were both busy in the field when a call came in to check on a doe hit by a car. It was going to be up to Flint to decide if the injured animal could be saved or if he should put it down on the spot.

The driver who had hit it was more worried about her dented car, which figured, since skittish white-tail deer were the scourge of the rural roads as well as the highways.

"She was standing over there in the bushes," the woman said, wringing her hands. "She didn't even try to run until I was right on top of her."

"Yeah, they do that," Flint said. "It wasn't your fault. These accidents happen all the time."

"I know. I was watching. I even slowed down, just in case, and she still plowed into my fender. My husband is going to kill me."

"At least she didn't dive through a window and tear you up with those sharp hooves," Flint said. "Do you want me to call a tow truck or are you okay to drive?"

"I'm okay. What about the deer?"

About time, Flint thought. "I'll take care of her. You're free to go."

"Thanks." The driver was mumbling as she headed for her car.

A closer examination of the groggy doe showed no broken bones that he could see without an X-ray, but he knew there could be internal injuries. He covered the doe's head with a sack while she was still stunned to keep her from panicking, then lifted her into the back of his truck, where she'd be secure for the short trip to Maggie's.

Maggie's. Just where he'd yearned to go. And now he had a valid reason for another visit. He'd been keeping watch during the night, making the excuse that his boss had assigned him to find Elwood and he expected to catch the old man visiting.

Taking it easy on the bumpy dirt and gravel roads for the sake of his passenger, Flint entered the long driveway to the compound. He'd have been happier if his pulse was not speeding like that of a teenager and his palms weren't getting sweaty. This was ridiculous. He was a grown man who had faced enemy combatants, yet here he was with his gut tied in knots over a pretty woman.

Flint saw her on the porch, watching, waiting. As soon as he circled the pickup and let down the tailgate, she hurried to join him.

"What have you got?"

"Deer versus Chevy. Can't tell who won yet."

"How long ago was she hit?"

"Probably less than an hour. She didn't lie in a ditch and suffer or anything. When I got there she seemed mostly stunned."

Maggie laid a gentling hand on the deer's side. "She's breathing normally. Let's get her into a holding pen so I can watch her move. I don't want to call Greg if I don't have to."

Flinching and trying to hide his telltale reaction to the other man's name, Flint sought to divert her attention. "Is Mark home yet?"

"No."

"When does he get out of school?"

"The bus usually drops him at the mailbox by three, but he won't be coming today."

Because Maggie had begun to slide the doe's forequarters toward the edge of the tailgate, Flint followed with the rear and positioned himself to lift the delicate animal. "I'll get her. You just show me where to put her."

As he followed past the house to the group of pens, Flint continued to probe. "Why isn't Mark coming home?"

He noticed movement of Maggie's shoulders, indicating a shrug and probably a sigh.

"My mother's going to be watching him all weekend," she said, holding open a narrow gate and gesturing. "Just put her in here and take off the hood as soon as I close the gate. If she bolts she's probably going to be okay."

"What made you decide to leave him with Faye?"

"Lots of things."

Noting that she kept her focus on the bewildered doe rather than look him in the eye, he continued to probe. "Like what? If you were going to move him to town, I'd have thought you'd have already done it."

"I probably should have." She finally raised her gaze to his face. "Have you heard any more about the truck that ran me off the road?"

"No. But I do want to talk to you about an assignment I've been given." He turned up the collar of his jacket against the biting wind. "Brrr."

Maggie laughed cynically. "If you want to be invited in, just ask. There's no need to pretend you're cold."

"I am cold," Flint countered. He eyed the sky. "Looks like it may snow soon."

"If it does it'll be one of the earliest snowfalls I can remember." She turned back to the house. "Come on. My new patient will calm down better if we're not hovering. We can keep an eye on her through the kitchen window."

"Got any coffee made?"

"No, but it won't take long. I'll put on a fresh pot."

As they climbed the back porch steps, he continued to look for answers about his son. "You never did explain why you suddenly decided to have Mark stay with your mom."

"Call it intuition," Maggie said.

"Did you hear wolves again?"

"No. That was part of the problem. I didn't hear anything. It was too quiet."

"What was your dog's reaction?"

"He wasn't out there with me. I'm keeping him shut up in Mark's room until I'm sure it's okay for him to run around on that sore foot."

"It's healing okay?"

"Yes. It looks terrible, but it's closing just like Greg promised."

"You like him, don't you?" *How did that get past my censors?* Flint wondered, disgusted with himself.

"Of course I do. He's been a lot of help with my animals. Ms. Dodd has been more than generous with her support. I just don't want to overspend on vet bills if I don't have to, and Greg is very fair."

"Right. Good. So, will Faye mind if I visit Mark at her house?"

Maggie began to smile. "Why don't you meet

me at Serenity Chapel Sunday morning and join us for pizza afterward at Mom's?"

"Really?"

"Really. Unless you're scared of the old-timers in the congregation."

"The only one who scares me is your uncle Elwood. I don't imagine he's been to any church in a while."

"Probably not. I do wish he'd let Robbie ride in with me, though."

"How far out does he live? I've heard three grandsons live with him. That must make it tough to get to town."

"Robbie walks or hitches rides. Luke and Will are both old enough to drive."

"I'd like to interview them. Any chance you could arrange it? If I have them picked up and hauled in, they'll be so mad they won't tell me a thing."

Maggie nodded. "You've got that right."

"How about the old man? Elwood. Do you know where I might find him?"

"I used to," Maggie replied. "Robbie just told me they've moved. I have no idea where they live now."

Flint didn't have to consult his notes to know who she meant. "He's the youngest, right?"

"Right. Robbie seems different. He's smart and pretty sensible, considering how he was raised. If any of the boys are redeemable, he is."

"Getting back to your uncle. What do you know about his hunting activities?" The somber look on her face told him she was aware of the man's reputation.

"He's always been a subsistence hunter," Maggie said. "At his age nobody's likely to change him." She hesitated as if making a decision, then went on. "If it hadn't been for Ira Crawford, my uncle would have lived a very different life. Just keep that in mind."

He scowled. "What are you talking about?"

"You must know the story. Ira stole Elwood's fiancée and his farm."

"That's ridiculous. He did nothing of the kind."

"Ask him."

"I will," Flint snapped back at her. But would he? Was it wise to rile the confused old man any more than he already had? The best recourse was probably to ask Bess, if he could do it casually. He certainly didn't want her to think he believed the impossible rumors that had circulated for generations. The more often those stories were retold, the more fantastic and unbelievable they became, until most folks totally rejected any hidden truths.

Staring at Maggie and noting her set jaw and raised chin, Flint figured he'd better back off before he made her so mad she tried to keep him away from his son. "So, is the coffee ready?"

He almost burst into laughter when her eyes widened in surprise. "Coffee?"

"Yes. Coffee. I distinctly recall being offered a cup."

To her credit she recovered quickly and crossed the room. "It's done. So, where do we stand on Sunday morning? I'll need to know how much pizza to order."

"Why don't you let me take care of the food while you and Faye look after Mark?"

Although she seemed surprised, she nevertheless agreed. "Okay. Mom and I like the supreme and Mark likes sausage. No mushrooms on his unless you want to listen to him wail."

"Got it."

Flint accepted the steaming mug she handed him and took a seat at the oak table. As soon as Maggie joined him he said, "So, what was so scary you sent the boy away? I'd have thought you'd do that right after the prowler incident."

"Like I said, I should have. But first I had to admit to myself that I wasn't invincible."

"And now?" Sipping coffee for something to do, he waited for her answer.

She said, "I need all the help I can get."

"Mine, too, I hope."

When she nodded and added, "*Especially* yours," Flint hid his grin behind the coffee mug and silently thanked the Lord for answered prayer. It wasn't always easy to see the good things that emerged from bad situations, but in this case he figured he did.

Circumstances had created a need, and he had arrived just in time to fill it. Doing so was bringing him back into Maggie's life and therefore into his son's. The sequence of events was pretty amazing.

And still dangerous, he reminded himself. It was all well and good to act the part of their protector—as long as he was successful. Failure was unthinkable.

Maggie had chosen a favorite, long-skirted dress with a crocheted shrug for Sunday. Deciding on shoes had been harder. She'd reasoned that heels would make it more difficult to run, so she'd stuck to flats.

That somber choice was disquieting. Here she was, ready for church, family and friends, yet she was still thinking about being able to flee. Her adversaries had done that to her and she didn't like it one bit.

Well, at least Mark would be spared her angst for a while. She'd made up her mind to let the boy stay with Faye a little longer. Mark could walk to school from her mother's house, but Faye, bless her heart, always insisted on driving him. Now that the weather was turning harsh, it was just as well anyway. But, oh, Maggie missed him.

A grin split her face as she left her truck and

headed toward the front of Serenity Chapel. There was her darling little boy, his hand held fast by his grandma to keep him from running to her across the busy parking lot. Faye waved. Maggie waved back, hurrying.

Then she saw him. Flint had come. But he wasn't standing with her mother and the boy, he was positioned next to one of the pillars that held up the overhang. His posture was stiff, his eyes scanning the lot as each vehicle arrived, and even though he wasn't in uniform he looked in total command.

Maggie greeted her mother and scooped up Mark, balancing him on her hip before approaching Flint.

"Good morning."

He nodded slightly. "Morning."

"How long have you been here?"

"Since about seven. Why?"

"That was what I was going to ask. Why?"

"Because it's the best way to be sure your relatives don't sneak in and cause trouble."

Maggie had to smile. "The church does have a security system. We lock the outside doors and volunteers watch for late arrivals."

"That won't do much good unless somebody looks dangerous and doesn't get let in. You and I know who to look out for, so I figured I'd watch."

"Thank you, but I really don't think it's necessary to stand guard duty. Why don't you come inside with us?"

He gave her a lopsided smile. "You're not afraid the roof will fall in?"

"I'll take my chances. Everybody's seen you out here as they drove by, so it won't exactly be a surprise."

"True. Pastor Malloy stuck his head out to greet me. I'm glad he's still here. He's a good preacher."

"Yes, he is. He really helped me after…" She glanced at Mark. "You know."

Flint was diverted long enough to tousle the boy's hair. "Hi, buddy. How's that mean old dog of yours?"

"He's not mean," Mark insisted.

"Just joking. Is his foot better?"

The child looked to his mother, so Maggie answered, "Much. I took the bandage off to let it breathe and it's healing well."

"Yeah," Mark said happily.

"I'm glad."

"Mom's working in the nursery today," Maggie said. "Come sit with us?"

"Doesn't Mark go with other kids?"

"Usually, we all come to Sunday school, but today we got a late start." She arched her eyebrows and met Flint's gaze, hoping he'd understand that she was really saying they'd decided to minimize the threat by limiting their time in public.

Judging by the wise look he returned, he got the picture. "And that's why you're taking the pizza home afterward?"

"Yes."

"Smart."

"We thought so." She started to turn, the child still balanced on one hip. "Come on. My passenger's getting heavy."

Flint held out his arms. "I can carry him for you."

She almost refused—would have if the tender expression on Flint's face had not touched her heart. When Mark put his arms out for Flint to take him, she gave in and relinquished the boy. "May as well. He looks more like you than he does me anyway."

As she finished speaking she noticed that Mark had been paying more attention than she'd expected. *Uh-oh.* He and Flint were staring into each other's eyes as if meeting for the first time.

"That's because we're both such handsome guys," Flint said, breaking eye contact. "Right, buddy?"

Mark giggled and hid his face against the shoulder of his father's sport jacket.

It was all Maggie could do to keep her tears at bay. All the rationalizing in the world was not enough to negate the guilt she felt for keeping these two apart.

Therefore, she had to figure out who was causing all the trouble and threatening their very lives. She simply had to. Because, one way or another, she was going to make sure her little boy got to know his real father the way he deserved to.

A shiver shot up her spine. She rapidly checked over both shoulders, seeing no problem. Was there one, or was she merely a victim of her own wayward imagination?

She hurried to match Flint's longer stride as he carried Mark into the sanctuary. "Let's sit in the corner over there," she said, touching his arm lightly and pointing. "We can see all the doors and nobody can get behind us."

"Now you're thinking sensibly," he said.

Maggie saw no reason to tell him she was keyed up. They all were, and for their own good. A complacent animal was easy prey. Clueless people were, too. They had to be on edge to keep their wits sharp and their senses honed.

Settling herself in the pew, she waited until Flint had placed Mark between them, then said, "I've changed my mind. I want you to teach me to shoot."

He arched an eyebrow. "What brought that on?"

"Rabbits," Maggie said, seeing him stifle a grin.

"Rabbits? Okay…"

"Think about it. They have no natural defenses except to run and hide from predators. I'm tired of being like them. I want some teeth and claws of my own so I can fight back."

"I'm not sure that's the right attitude. Aggression can get you into trouble."

"So can freezing like a deer caught in a car's headlights."

"Speaking of that, how's your latest patient?"

"Fine. Don't try to change the subject."

"Wouldn't dream of it. When do you want these lessons?"

She leaned closer to speak over Mark's head while he busied himself pretending to read the Sunday bulletin. "Soon as possible." She eyed the boy. "I'm going to let Mom keep taking care of him for a while, so now would be a good time."

"How about this evening?"

It suddenly occurred to Maggie that she'd invited the love of her life to visit her at home while she was alone. Not the smartest thing she'd ever done. It was, however, the best opportunity for her to practice shooting, so she agreed.

"Fine. After we eat at Mom's I'll go on home to do my chores and you can drop by. Any time before dark will be fine. I have a .38 revolver that was Dad's. I've never shot it. He tried to teach me before he got so sick, but I was too afraid."

"If you find you're still scared, we'll have to do something else to help you feel safe, like maybe get you a Taser," Flint said. "Nobody should try to handle a gun unless they're confident and capable."

"I've changed a lot since I was a kid," Maggie countered. "There is nothing I can't do once I set my mind to it."

Flint looked down at the well-behaved child between them and smiled. "I believe you."

TWELVE

The leisure time Flint shared with his son and the women flew by. If he'd had his choice, Maggie would not have insisted on going home alone. She stubbornly rejected the idea of letting him accompany her even though her own mother urged it.

"All I'm going to do is my usual chores, just like every other day. Wolfie will warn me if there's a problem."

"And chase off a dangerous pack of wolves?" Faye asked.

"If necessary. Flint never did find any sign of predators when Wolfie got hurt, so there's a good chance there never were any. Everybody knows a trapper like Elwood can make animal noises better than most animals can. I sure wouldn't put it past him to do it to scare me. Or to try to stir up trouble."

"That would explain the boot prints I found,"

Flint said. "Is he likely to have doctored your dog for you?"

Maggie said, "No" without hesitation. "But Robbie might have." She made a silly face. "And, no, I did not put him up to tying Wolfie to a tree so one of the Witherspoons could shoot a Crawford, okay?"

"I never really thought you did. I was just…"

"Mad at me. I know. You had good reason." She paused, checking to make sure her son was playing with the dog instead of listening. "But try to see it from my side. You left Serenity without a word and I didn't hear from you afterward. Why should I have tried to find you to tell you about Mark?"

Scowling, Flint looked first at Faye, then back to Maggie. "I left you a note. And I wrote letters, at least in the beginning."

"You never."

"Ask your mother."

Both of them faced Faye, whose cheeks and nose had turned the color of a bad sunburn. "It wasn't my doing."

"Mother!"

Teary-eyed and wringing her hands, Faye tried to explain. "You know how your father could be. He was as hateful as the rest of my kin—and he'd only married into our feud. Everybody kept insisting that you were better off without Flint. After a while I guess I started to believe it."

"Why didn't you *tell* me?"

"You and Mark filled a terrible void in my life after Frank died, and I knew if I fessed up you were liable to leave me all alone."

"I don't believe this." Looking stunned, Maggie turned to Flint. "I'm so sorry. I thought you were glad to be rid of me."

"You couldn't have *asked* me?"

"How? I knew you'd joined the service, but that was all. I didn't even know which branch at first."

"Bess and Ira did. You could have approached them."

"With a baby in my arms? That would have gone over like a lead balloon. Besides, what makes you think they'd have told me?"

"Bess would have, at least back then. Now I'm not so sure. Ira has turned into a mean old cuss since I've been gone. And she tends to back him up, even if he's wrong."

"I'm sorry about that, too," Maggie said, "but at least his failings brought you back."

"There is that." Flint smiled. "Romans 8:28?"

"Yes. 'All things work together for good for those who love God and are called according to His purpose.'" Making a face, Maggie gathered up her purse and called to Mark. "Come on, honey. Time to go."

Flint put out a hand. "Hold it. I thought you were going to leave him here."

"That was when I thought I could trust my own mother," Maggie replied. She smiled at him. "Why don't you just follow us home and spend the rest of the day? I'm sure we can work out a way to practice gun handling safely. After all, I'll have to keep the gun in an accessible place as soon as I'm sure of myself."

He helped her on with her jacket, then did the same for his son. Such simple kindnesses, yet they made him feel so good, almost as if he were part of a real family. That was the kind of closeness that had been missing in his life ever since he was a kid. Great-grandparents Bess and Ira had given him a home, yes, but they had never made him feel as if he belonged. Although that was probably at least partially due to their disappointment in both his mother and grandmother, it didn't make up for the emotional alienation.

Perhaps that was what had drawn him to Maggie so strongly. She had a loving heart, the kind that had led her to care for helpless animals when she could have made a lot more money doing just about anything else.

He followed as Maggie led the way to the door. Mark was in her arms, waving goodbye. Faye just stood there with both hands clamped over her mouth as if trying to hold back sobs. Yes, he felt sorry for the older woman. Anybody would. But there was more to his feelings than that. Hiding the truth just to have her own way had cost Faye dearly, and she was now paying for those lies.

And she wasn't the only one. The pain and astonishment in Maggie's expression when she'd learned about his letters had proven her innocence without a doubt. Too bad he had accused her of lying about his efforts to contact her when *she* was the one who had been lied to.

Flint followed her and Mark out onto the porch and slipped his arm around her shoulders when she seemed to falter. "Are you okay?"

Maggie shook her head. "No. I don't think I'll ever be okay again." Her lower lip was quivering.

Flint tightened his hold and she turned into his embrace, holding their son as the third side of the triangle.

Mark instinctively put his little arms around his parents' necks. "Don't cry, Mama."

When she didn't answer, Flint began to stroke her silky hair, meaning only to comfort and belatedly realizing how much he'd wanted to touch her ever since the first moment he saw her again.

This embrace was different from the temporary closeness they'd shared after her accident. This was all of them together. His family. There might never be a legal binding, but that wouldn't change his certainty that the three of them belonged together.

They always had.

* * *

Maggie was torn between the knowledge that her heavenly Father expected her to forgive Faye and a terrible sense of betrayal. All this time she'd been blaming Flint for deserting her and he hadn't done so. Little wonder he'd been so angry when he first saw Mark.

Laying her cheek against Flint's shoulder, she fought to regain her self-control. It did no good to keep telling herself to pull away when this was exactly where she wanted to be. In his arms. Close enough to pretend they had never been estranged or belonged to extended families that hated each other. *Ha!* That would be the day.

Now that she knew what had happened between Ira and Elwood all those years ago, she couldn't see any solution short of moving away and changing her name. Come to think of it, that wasn't such a bad idea.

She eased back to look up at Flint and almost came undone again when she saw the glint of unshed tears in his emerald eyes. The poor man was suffering and it was all her fault.

Instead of commiserating, she decided to try to lighten the mood by sharing her random thoughts. "I think I'd like to be Maggie Gilhooley. How does that sound?"

He frowned. "What?"

"When we change our names and escape from this crazy town," Maggie explained. Eyes widening, she went on. "No. Mulrooney. That sounds better with Maggie. Maggie Mulrooney. What do you think?"

"I think you've had a rough day and maybe OD'd on pizza." He shifted to stand beside her and ushered her to her truck. "Get in. I'll follow you home."

"No."

"No?"

"No." The snap decision was so right it made her heart swell. "First you need to take the booster seat out of my truck and put it in yours so Mark can ride with you."

"Really?"

The child cheered. "Yeah!"

"Okay, if you say so," Flint agreed. "Give me a second to stow the laptop and move the rest of my gear to make room."

As Maggie stood by with their son, she sensed a growing peace. Much of her world was in upheaval, yet she had just taken the first step toward making things right. There was no way to go back and change the past, of course, but she could begin to foster healing.

"There. All set," Flint said, straightening and holding out his arms. "Ready, Mark?"

"Yeah. Can I blow the siren?"

"How about just the lights for now? We can save the siren for a better time."

His little mouth puckered, but he conceded. "Oh, okay."

Maggie had to smile at the exchange. It looked as if Mark had met his match. So had Flint. They were so alike it was amazing. And equally stubborn. Not that Mark had inherited any traits like that from her.

The boy was seated and buckled in before she turned toward her truck. And froze. A noisy International pickup was cruising by in the street. It was red. And rusty.

She spun and raced back to Flint, pointing and waving her arms. "There! Look!"

By the time he paid attention to her frantic gestures, it was too late. The truck was gone.

"Did you see that?"

"See what?"

"Elwood's truck. It just drove by. If you hurry, maybe you can catch him."

Flint eyed his son. "Not with Mark along. Did you see which way he was headed?"

"Downtown."

"Okay. Stick with me. I'll cruise that way before we head out to your place. But no car chases. Promise?"

"Promise. Do you think he's stalking us?"

"Let's try to find out."

Flint took extra care traveling through town. So far, Maggie was behaving herself. If the emotional upheaval they had both experienced was affecting her as much as it was him, he'd understand if she acted a little overwrought.

They were passing the town market. Flint heard a horn honk. Maggie was waving an arm out the window, obviously trying to get his attention, so he pulled over.

Parking right behind him, she jumped down and approached at a trot, pointing. "There. That's his truck. He's at the market."

"All right. You get in with Mark and lock the doors while I go see."

"Do you know what he looks like these days?"

"Close enough. I've seen mug shots of the two older grandsons, and from what we've gathered, Elwood looks pretty wild. He has a gray beard and messy, long hair."

"Right. I've heard he's really let himself go." She reached for his arm. "Be careful."

"I just want to talk to him. I can't arrest him unless I can prove he's been poaching."

"Prove it? How?"

"By catching him in the act or finding too much deer meat in his freezer and a pile of discarded hide and antlers like the one I found on Nine Mile Ridge recently."

"Wait! You can't arrest him?"

"Not without good cause. Looking dangerous isn't a crime."

"Well, it should be."

Flint waited until he was certain she'd locked the truck doors, then headed for the grocery store. Judging by so few cars, there weren't many shoppers on Sunday.

Instead of entering the store and taking a chance of creating trouble inside, he leaned against the rusty old truck and waited. The two men who soon approached were scruffy but definitely not Elwood.

Flint smiled slightly and nodded a greeting. "Evening, boys. You must be Luke and Will."

Luke, the taller of the two, scowled beneath the brim of a dirty baseball cap. "Who's askin'?"

"Is this your grandpa's truck?"

"I said, who're you?"

Continuing to smile, Flint offered his hand. "I'm surprised you don't recognize me."

Will started to reach out to shake. His brother elbowed to stop him. "Don't. It's that new game warden."

"Right you are." Flint looked past them. "You two alone tonight?"

"What's it to ya?"

"Just wondering. I'd really like to talk to Elwood."

Both young men chuckled. Will muttered, "Yeah, I bet you would."

"There'll be no trouble as long as you stick to the rules," Flint said amiably. "We all want the deer population to stay healthy. That's why Game and Fish sets limits and seasons."

"Don't lecture us, Crawford," Luke said with a sneer. "Witherspoons have been huntin' these deer woods for a lot longer than you've been alive."

"True. And we're coming up on modern gun season, so I won't be giving you any trouble about what weapons you choose. But I do need to warn you about taking too many bucks or shooting does."

"Meat's meat," Luke countered. He shouldered Flint aside to yank open the driver's door of the old truck while Will circled to the passenger side.

Flint tried to hand Luke a business card. "Have Elwood call me, will you? I'll be glad to drive out to wherever he's living and meet with him any time."

The card fluttered to the pavement. Both young men were laughing as they drove away.

Flint jogged back across the street. Maggie stepped out, waiting by the open door of his truck. "How did it go?"

"As well as can be expected."

"That good, huh?"

He realized she was trying to joke. "Almost."

"Did they mention me?"

"Come to think of it, no," Flint said, thoughtful. "Are you ready to head to the sanctuary?"

"Yes. Let's get home while we still have daylight. I'll do chores and you can check the house for me."

"And then teach you to shoot?"

"Yes. I've actually handled a rifle a few times before. My dad showed me how. But that's no guarantee I'll know how to stay safe with a handgun. It's not the same thing."

"Precisely."

"I hope you're duly impressed with my sensible choices," she said. "I'd hate to think you still see me as a silly teenager."

"You were never silly," Flint countered. "Stubborn, hardheaded and a lot prettier than you thought, but never silly."

"Was that a compliment?"

"It was supposed to be."

"Good. Let's get out of here before those guys decide to come back and cause us trouble."

"We can't use the lights when we're in traffic," Flint told Mark. "Wait till we get to your driveway and we can do it again."

"Why?"

"Because it will confuse other drivers."

"Why?"

"Because lights are for emergencies."

"Why?"

Studying the child's impish expression, Flint realized he'd been had. As soon as he chuckled, Mark covered his mouth and began to giggle.

"Do you do that to your mother, too?" Flint asked.

"Uh-huh. All the time. She says I'm smart."

"She's right."

"Are you gonna marry her?"

It took Flint a couple of seconds to close his mouth and answer, "Why?" which triggered more giggles.

Mark sobered. "I think she likes you."

"I like her, too."

"That's good, huh?"

Reaching over to pat his son on the knee, he said, "Yes. That's very good."

The boy suddenly seemed distracted. Flint had been keeping such a close eye on Maggie's truck he'd failed to notice a column of smoke in the distance. When Mark pointed, it was clear.

Flint grabbed his phone. Maggie didn't answer his call, but judging by the way she sped up she'd seen the smoke, too. He alerted the sheriff and fire department, then flipped on his lights and siren.

"Yeah! Can we go real fast, too, like Mama?"

"Maybe not quite that fast," Flint said, "but we'll get there. I want you to be safe."

"I got my seat belt on. See?"

"Yes, but even a seat belt isn't enough in a bad accident."

Just when he thought he was having a sensible father-and-son conversation and imparting important knowledge, he heard a giggle. "Why?"

It did occur to Flint to actually explain, but he decided to save that for a later time. Right now his main goal had to be getting to Maggie's and helping her put out the fire before she got herself hurt trying to be too brave. She would. He knew she would. When the health and safety of a helpless animal was at stake, there was no doubt.

With Mark cheering and the truck bouncing over the potholes in the dirt drive, they drew closer. Thankfully, the smoke wasn't coming from the house, nor was there much fire out by the barn. That was a better scenario than he'd first expected.

"Okay," Flint said, skidding to a stop and pulling his keys from the ignition. "You'll be safe out here. Stay in the truck while I go help your mother. You hear?"

"Wh—" The child apparently noted his stern expression and stopped teasing. He bowed his head instead and said, "Okay."

"Promise?"

"Uh-huh."

Flint had no choice but to trust him. Hitting the ground running, he pushed the button on his key fob to lock the truck doors, then began to pray as he searched for Maggie.

All he could manage was a heartfelt "Please, Lord," but he figured, under the circumstances, that was plenty.

THIRTEEN

Most of the pile of loose straw was smoldering while flames danced at the edges. Maggie grabbed a hose and began to wet down the bales behind the fire to keep it from spreading.

She heard Flint shout, "Fire department's coming," as he wielded a pitchfork to clear a path between the burning straw and her winter hay storage.

"Where's Mark?" she screeched at him.

"In my truck."

"Safe?"

"As safe as I could make him."

"We need Wolfie," she shouted back before throwing down the hose. "Have you got this?"

"Yeah. Go get the dog. I'll finish here and then check the rest of the yard."

In the panic of the moment, she hadn't thought about anything but quenching the flames. Now that she was on the move, she realized Flint was right. Just because they'd put out one fire didn't mean the danger was past.

Her house was supposed to be locked up tight, so when she found the rear door ajar it startled her. "Wolfie!"

The big dog crawled out from under the kitchen table and hurried to her, slightly favoring his cut paw.

Instead of entering the house, Maggie led him around to the front looking for the Game and Fish truck. Mark was on his knees, peering out a side window, but he'd stayed put despite the excitement. When he saw Maggie and their dog he scrunched up his face and burst into tears.

She gave the door handle a jerk. Nothing happened. "It's locked, honey. You'll have to open it from the inside."

Mark was still shedding tears, but he shook his head.

"Come on, honey. It's okay. Open the door."

Still, the child resisted. Maggie began to scowl. "What's the matter? Why can't you open it?"

Mark pointed to where the smoke was dissipating. The truth struck her like a physical blow. He was obeying his father's orders instead of listening to hers.

Calm down, she told herself. *Get a grip. It's not the end of the world.*

But it was the end of her total control, she realized sadly. Not only was she going to have to share the raising of Mark, but she was going to have to adjust to having Flint in her life in a big, big way, like it or not. She'd coped alone for so long it had become second nature, yet when it came to defending herself and her child, she had to admit it was comforting to have an ally.

Speaking of whom... Flint was rounding the house, gun drawn, and looking every bit like a commando despite wearing church clothes. When he noticed her standing by his truck, she motioned and he unlocked the doors remotely.

"Did you leave the back door open?" he asked as she helped Mark down.

"No. That's how I found it. I was really careful after that prowler incident. I know I locked everything before I left this morning."

"Okay. You stay here so you can talk to the firefighters. I'll circle around back to make sure nobody lights another fire."

"The arsonists must be long gone," Maggie insisted. She reached for his arm to stop him. "Wolfie was hiding under the kitchen table. If a stranger had been in or near the house, he wouldn't have done that."

"Suppose it was somebody he knew?" Flint argued. "Maybe cousin Robbie came back."

"He'd never break into my house." Maggie was certain of it. "Like I've said before, Elwood is a bad influence. Robbie's okay, but..." She gasped. "Wait a minute. We saw Luke and Will in town.

They couldn't have gotten here, started this fire and escaped. We'd have seen them."

She noted that Flint had stationed himself with his back to her and Mark, becoming a human shield. Sirens in the distance were not nearly as comforting as knowing that this man intended to defend her totally.

Touching his shoulder, Maggie said, "Thank you."

"I'd normally say, 'My pleasure,' but that doesn't fit this occasion."

She mustered her courage. "What if Elwood is not the one responsible?"

"Then the sheriff and I will pin it on whoever is guilty."

"It can't be Robbie. He would never do anything to harm me."

Beneath her soft touch she felt his shoulder stiffen. "Who else is there?" He turned.

"I don't know, unless Abigail's niece and nephew are still on the warpath. She's been considering having the house redone and they may not want her to spend the money."

"It makes no sense to burn it down."

"Sure it does. No house, no expense. And probably no wild animal sanctuary, either."

"Do you think they'd stoop to committing actual crimes?"

"They might. Greed is a great incentive."

"True."

"So is hatred," Maggie went on. "Elwood isn't the only one who might be nurturing that old grudge or be unhappy that you and I have been together so much. We've been concentrating on Witherspoons. How about broadening our suspicions to include Crawfords?"

"What?" The response was so harsh Mark hid behind his mother's leg and Wolfie growled.

"You heard me." She stood firm, chin raised. "Just because there aren't many Crawfords left doesn't mean they aren't as angry as Elwood."

"The only ones left around here are my grandparents. Are you implying that a sweet old woman and a man who can barely remember how to tie his own shoes are out to get you just because of your lineage?" He huffed. "Now I've heard everything."

Maggie backed down. "Ira's that bad? I'm sorry. I didn't know."

"Yeah, he's that bad. He also thinks I'm trying to steal his farm from him."

"Are you sure?"

"Positive. I overheard him ranting about it."

"That's interesting," she said, watching the fire engine and a sheriff's car stop next to her house and Flint hurry toward the men who were getting out.

It was probably for the best that this particular discussion was over. If it had continued, Maggie feared, she might have overstepped and suggested that Ira's guilty conscience was making him imagine payback in kind for his long-ago sins.

That was half the trouble with holding grudges, she decided. The person who remained angry wasn't the only one who suffered. Both sides did, as well as those around them who absorbed the rancor. What a waste. There was no telling how many lives had been ruined in the past or might be harmed in the future from Ira Crawford's betrayal of his friends. Truth to tell, just because some of his and Elwood's descendants weren't vocal about their prejudices was no proof they were innocent. Considering the feud in that light greatly increased the suspect pool.

Maggie shivered as those details settled in her heart and mind. A good third of the town was related to one side or the other, which made a lot of her friends and acquaintances persons of interest.

That was scary.

It was late afternoon before the professionals on scene finished trading "war" stories and went their separate ways. The practice of unwinding after facing a tense situation was common and served to help fire and police alike to decompress. The same kind of kinship had occurred after combat missions. Reminiscing about his time in the service, however, was not something

Flint enjoyed. He'd done his duty. As far as he was concerned, that part of his life was over.

He huffed. *Yeah*. Except that while he was away his family had been formed. Without him. If he'd even suspected that he'd be needed at home, he'd never have left.

Although he tended to blame Maggie for refusing to marry him, his decision to go had not been totally her fault. His grandparents' negative attitudes had also contributed. Looking back, he could see that Ira had already been showing signs of dementia then. Signs he'd managed to hide behind irrational anger and bluster.

Could Maggie's notion about the Crawfords be right? Flint shook his head decisively. *No*. Shirttail relatives were unconcerned. And Ira? Flint couldn't wrap his mind around that concept no matter how ill the old man was.

The wildlife compound seemed awfully quiet once the others were gone. Flint kept a close eye on their surroundings as well as staying near Mark. It was satisfying to see how intelligent and inquisitive the boy was and flattering to be the recipient of a long string of questions, usually followed by "Why?"

Maggie was closing the last pen when Flint approached her. "Chores done?"

"For now." She eyed the darkening sky. "If it snows I may need to add more bedding, but I don't want to jump the gun."

"Speaking of guns," Flint said, smiling slightly, "when do you want your first lesson?"

Her momentary hesitation was expected. So was the deep sigh. "I don't know. All that running around and worry really tired me out."

"I know. How about an afternoon snack?" He eyed Mark. "Then Wolfie can watch cartoons with his favorite friend."

"While we go out in the yard to shoot. Great idea. I have apples in the fridge and cookies in the cupboard."

"Not to worry," Flint said, smiling. "When I picked up the pizza I bought dessert. It's out in my truck."

Maggie rolled her eyes while Mark jumped up and down and cheered. "Don't tell me. You got those sticky, frosted dough things that are a nutritional disaster."

"Yup. We can talk about healthy food another day. Right now it's empty calorie time."

"You're spoiling us."

His smile grew to a face-splitting grin. "I hope so."

Although she led the way into the kitchen, he could tell she wasn't enthusiastic. Was she sorry she'd asked him to stay? Was she afraid of shooting? If she was truly as weary as she was acting, perhaps it would be best to postpone her lesson.

"Mark and I will wash up while you go get our dessert," Maggie told him. "Coffee, too?"

"Sure. Thanks." Flint started through the house heading for the front door. He and the sheriff had both checked all the rooms, but that wasn't enough to generate calm. Or peace. And if he felt uneasy in that old house, how must Maggie feel, particularly at night when she was alone?

Not exactly alone, he added, stepping up the pace to get back to her ASAP. She had the dog to help keep watch and a boy—his boy—to keep safe. The burden of being a single parent must be immense. No wonder she seemed uptight much of the time.

Something about his truck seemed off. Flint frowned as he reached to open the door. Once inside, he could tell what was wrong when he moved aside his notebook and the pen rolled away.

He circled the vehicle with the box of sticky bread in his hands. Two of his tires had been flattened. Closer inspection showed no damage, and he hoped a simple airing-up would fix the problem.

Flint jogged back to the house and ducked in the door, slamming it behind him.

"What's wrong?"

He'd hoped to hide his anxiety. He'd failed. One look at Maggie and he knew she had sensed a problem. "Flat tires on my truck," he said. "Unless you have an air compressor, I'm going to need to call a tow truck."

"No. Sorry. What happened to them?"

"Looks like a vandal let the air out on the side opposite the house, where we couldn't see him doing it," Flint said. He set the confection box in the center of the kitchen table.

Maggie was frowning as she brought their drinks and placed a glass of milk in front of her son. "That's illogical."

"Why?" Realizing who he sounded like, he winked at the child.

"Because. If somebody wants to get rid of you, why would they try to make you stay?" She arched an eyebrow. "You didn't mess with your own tires, did you?"

"And strand myself? Don't be ridiculous."

"Okay. I had to ask."

"No, you didn't." He willed her to understand that his motives were pure. "You and I need to make a pact to be nothing but truthful with each other. There's already been too much held back, too much misunderstanding. That ends right now." He offered his hand. "Agreed?"

Hesitating, Maggie stared at his hand for what seemed like hours before she reached for it and said, "Agreed."

Flint had meant to merely shake on their mutual promise, but the moment his hand touched

Maggie's, all previous notions fled like a startled covey of quail.

Their gazes met. Held. Flint tried to read her thoughts and found himself drowning in waves of emotion. She began to tremble. He covered their clasped hands with his other, drawing on the warmth of her delicate fingers and yearning to wrap her in a long embrace.

Do it, his heart urged. *Just do it.* Did he dare? Was it too soon, or would *any* time be wrong? Flint knew Maggie loved their son and had once loved him, or so she'd said. If he was going to honor their pledge, perhaps now was the time to begin airing the truth.

What *was* the truth? he asked himself. Did he love her the same way he used to? No. They had both changed too much over time. So, was that a problem? Perhaps. And what about her feelings? If she was still struggling to forgive him, despite her mother's confession about destroying his letters, was she ready to discuss possibilities for a shared future? Sharing parental responsibility was one thing. Recommitting to each other was decidedly different.

"Mama?" Mark whined. "I'm hungry."

That was enough to break into Flint's spinning, soaring thoughts and bring him back down to earth. He released his hold just as Maggie jerked her hand away.

"Me, too, honey," she said, fussing with a napkin before tucking it into the neck of Mark's shirt. "You still have your Sunday clothes on and I don't want you to get them all sticky."

"Aw, Mama."

Flint had to smile. His son was not merely a typical boy; he was the kind of kid who looked so cute while misbehaving that it was going to be hard to discipline him properly. "Don't argue with your mother," Flint said, trying to keep a straight face despite Mark's pout. "She's boss."

"Uh-uh. I'm the man of the house."

A fleeting glance at Maggie told him she'd put that idea in the boy's head. "Men are a bit taller and older," Flint said to him gently. "Kind of like me. When you get as big as I am, then you can be the man of the house." Lack of verbal contradiction from Maggie gave him the courage to add, "In the meantime, I'll help. Okay?"

Mark had time for only "Okay" before he stuck the sticky bread in his mouth and began to chew.

"You think I was wrong, don't you?" she asked.

"It's not my place to judge. I just think that's a heavy responsibility for a little guy, that's all. Let him be a kid, Maggie. Don't try to make him grow up too fast."

"There you go again," she countered, hands fisted on her hips. "First you tell me I'm doing a good job, then you turn around and criticize."

"Truth, remember?" Judging by the way she

rolled her eyes and tossed her head, she'd had enough truth for a while.

"You stay here and watch your…Mark. I'm going to go change for my shooting lesson."

"Fine by me." Sliding into a chair next to the boy, Flint helped himself to sticky bread. Maggie was right. It was all sugar and carbs. Oh, well. Once in a while wasn't going to hurt. Mark was obviously enjoying his treat, so buying the stuff had been a good idea. Sort of.

He was at the kitchen sink, wetting a paper towel to clean the boy's hands, when he heard Maggie shout.

"Flint! Come here."

Milk spilled when he scooped up Mark and took him along. There was no sign of Maggie in the first bedroom, but he could tell it was hers from the dress left lying on the bed. "Where are you?"

"Mark's room."

With the child tucked behind him, Flint led the way into the room. It looked ransacked, but that wasn't new. It had looked that way when he and the sheriff checked it and were assured it was usually messy.

"What's wrong?"

"The window."

Flint bent to peer at it. "It looks okay."

Maggie pointed with a shaky finger. "The glass does. The screen is missing."

"Maybe it just fell out. This is an old house."

"Yes, it is," Maggie replied. "It's so old that most of the windows stick after being repainted so many times and the screens are so warped they're nailed in."

"Somebody pulled nails to get it off?" His pulse had been rapid when she called to him. Now his heart felt as if it might pound through the walls of his chest any moment. "We should call Harlan."

"No. Not again. Don't you see? The more often I report a minor crime, the more fed up he and his men are going to get. Pretty soon they won't even want to make a run out here, let alone do it in a hurry. I think that's part of the stalker's plan."

"That's paranoid."

"Only if nobody is after me."

Flint nodded and added, "Us. After us."

For once he wished Maggie would argue.

FOURTEEN

Maggie surprised herself as a marksman but only did well when Flint loaded and cocked the handgun for her. Otherwise, she felt inept and unsure.

"I can see it's going to take more practice before I'm proficient," she said.

"Afraid so. Which makes my decision easier."

Looking at him from the side, she knew she was scowling and made no effort to stop. "What decision?"

"The one I made when I found my tires flattened. I'm staying."

If he hadn't held up a hand to silence her, she would have interrupted before he added, "I'll bunk on the floor in Mark's room. You won't even notice me."

That'll be the day. "No way. When is the tow truck coming to put air in your tires?"

"Sometime before dark tonight. I told him to take his time so we'd have a chance to shoot before he got here and interrupted us. You did want a lesson, didn't you?"

"You know I did." Frustration with everything made her grumpy. "I'm surprised you were willing to stand in the yard with me, especially after you made me wear your bulletproof vest."

"I've been thinking—" he began.

Maggie interrupted. "So have I, and I've come to the conclusion that whoever is causing all the trouble has blown plenty of chances to do serious harm. Maybe they don't really want to hurt anybody."

"Maybe. I still don't intend to leave my son unprotected until this mystery is solved."

She started to say, *He's my son*, then stopped herself. Flint had a perfect right to act on Mark's behalf. What she didn't like acknowledging was the relief she felt knowing he was going to stay close by.

"All right." Thinking of the logistics, Maggie smiled. "Um, would you like me to get some blankets and make you a pallet on the floor or will you just bunk with Wolfie?"

"I carry a sleeping bag and camping equipment in my truck. I'll make do on my own."

"Okay." She'd expected more of a quip out of him but decided there was nothing wrong with being serious. She knew how scared she'd been during the other attacks and had only resorted to humor this time to lighten her own mood. "What will we tell Mark?"

"I don't know. What do you usually tell him when you have company?"

"The only overnight company I've had is when I was sick and Mom stayed with us a few days." Maggie pulled a face. "I suppose I should call and talk to her, but I get so mad when I think about what she did, I doubt I could be civil."

"Then take your time. Work through it," Flint said. He picked up the gun she'd been using, dropped the clip out and levered the last shell from the chamber before handing it to her.

"I need to lock this up somewhere."

"Yes. For now, I'll keep the ammo so it's separate from the gun until we get you a lockbox. No matter how well behaved you think a kid is, they're curious."

"Especially *ours*," she said, surprised when expressing shared parenthood felt right. Clearly, Flint noticed, because she saw him pause for a moment before going to his truck to stash the ammo and get his sleeping bag. By the time he tossed the roll on his shoulder and turned back to face her, however, there was no sign of uneasiness.

Except for mine, she mused, disgusted with herself. Her life had had other confusing and trying events that she'd managed beautifully, at least in the long run. Since Flint had returned, nothing had been simple or clear-cut. Not only were her nerves frayed, but her emotional condition was reduced to a rubble of its former sturdiness.

In silent prayer for wisdom and peace, she followed Flint back into the house and locked the door behind them. This night promised to be the longest, most difficult of her life, yet if enduring it would safeguard her little boy, she'd hang in there. No matter what.

And no matter how much rumor and innuendo she had to endure in the future, she added. Sadly, there was nothing romantic left between her and Flint—and she trusted him implicitly—so she wasn't worried on that score. She'd kept her chin up as an unwed mother. She could stand strong again.

The only aspect that truly bothered her was the nasty names some of the other kids had called poor Mark. He might not know what they'd meant yet, but it wouldn't be long before one of those bigger boys explained it to him.

All she could do was love him unconditionally and teach him that he was a gift from God. Which he was. People made mistakes, but their heavenly Father never did. He'd given her a beautiful son and she was blessed. Period.

The natural progression of that affirmation of faith led her to think of Flint Crawford; not as he once was but as the man he'd become. If God had sent him back to her to help protect Mark, fine.

On the other hand, if there was more to his abrupt arrival in Serenity, she was going to have to come to terms with a lot of things, not the least of which was her own heart. The two of them were burdened with enough excess baggage to fill the cargo hold of a passenger jet.

And, if she was assuming correctly, at least one of those theoretical bags had the potential to be deadly. She didn't know what was worse, worrying about an attack or wondering if they'd escape once it occurred.

"One day at a time," Flint said amiably after she'd mentioned her concerns. "Don't borrow trouble. Tomorrow, when it's daylight, I'll poke around outside and see what clues I can turn up. It's possible those old nails holding the screen just rusted away."

"All at once? On only *his* window?"

Flint lifted his shoulders and struck a nonchalant pose. At least he thought he did. If Maggie hadn't reacted so strongly initially, he'd have been happier. Saying, "Relax. I've got this," didn't help a whole lot, and her nervousness was rubbing off on him.

"Why don't you keep chilling on the couch while I bring in extra wood for the fireplace?" he said. "The weather's supposed to turn tonight."

"I have plenty of wood inside," she argued. "I can take care of myself."

"*Without* my help."

"Look. I'm sorry. It's just that every time you offer to do something like that it makes me feel as if you think I'm not capable."

"What gave you that idea?"

"I don't know. Coping by myself, I guess. Mom was dead set against my taking this job and moving out here. She kept nagging me about getting stuck in the middle of nowhere. I still doubt she believes I'll succeed."

"Is that why you're out here? You're escaping?"

To his relief, Maggie smiled slightly and shook her head. "Not primarily. I went to school to be a vet tech, but there weren't any local jobs and I needed to stay near Mom. When Abigail Dodd offered me a chance to work with wild animals and a house to live in, I jumped at the offer." She spread her arms wide and leaned against the back of the sofa while Mark's head rested in her lap and the dog lay at her feet.

"Gotcha." Flint wished he could find something constructive to do other than just watch TV or tend the fire. Being idle gave him too much time to think. About Maggie. About his son. Amazingly, he already loved that kid.

What about the boy's mama? Flint asked himself. Did he love her, too? Maybe. Probably. Just not the way he had as a teenager. The feelings he now had for Maggie were different. Deeper.

Surer. With a lot less immediacy and a lot more patience. If he asked her to elope today and she refused, he'd find another solution. A better one.

But first things first. They had to stick together for the common good and solve the puzzle of who was causing them so much grief. Until recently there had been no direct threat to Mark, but that had changed. Maggie had surprised a prowler in the boy's room and now a window screen was down. Either aspect deserved extra concern.

Flint stuck his pistol in the waistband of his dress pants and pulled his heavier work jacket on over his sport coat before adding a hat. "I'm going to patrol the yard. Be back in a few minutes."

She stiffened. "Why? Did you hear something?"

"No. It just makes sense to look around out there. You never know. I might stumble on another prowler."

"Be careful."

Mimicking a salute, he smiled down on his dozing son. "I will. You take care of him."

Maggie's "Always" was tender and softly spoken.

Flint opened the front door and stopped. "It's snowing. Do we need to do anything more for your animals?"

"Not tonight. They have plenty of bedding to

keep warm. In the morning we can add more if we need to."

"Okay. Keep that fire going." Although he knew she would, he felt he needed to say something else in parting. He'd chosen to inspect the property simply to relieve the tension from being around her, yet he hated to actually let her out of his sight.

Standing at the edge of the porch, he tucked the cuffs of his slacks into the tops of his boots and pondered the possible effects of the impending storm. It was early in the year for snow, so it probably wouldn't be deep or last long. Still, any weather change called for sensible precautions.

They had plenty of food and bottled water in the house. He knew because he'd checked. And the sheds outside held sacks of special animal preparations for omnivores as well as straight herbivores like the white-tailed deer.

Flint stepped off the porch and rounded the corner of the house, already leaving tracks in the fluff of snow. There was not enough to crunch or squeak underfoot yet, so it muffled his steps.

Movement ahead caught his attention. He squinted into the flurries. Drew his sidearm and rested his thumb on the safety. Someone was rifling through the cabinet where Maggie stored her vet supplies.

He tiptoed closer. The thief froze in midmotion. So did Flint. The tableau seemed to last forever before the thief turned to look over his shoulder and spotted him.

"Freeze," Flint shouted, taking a shooter's stance and wishing he was in full uniform. "Officer of the law."

Mumbled curses echoed. The man called out.

Flint pressed his back to the biggest oak in Maggie's yard and braced himself. If attacked, he intended to give as good as he got.

The person near the medicine cabinet ducked and began to flee.

"Stop or I'll shoot!" Flint ordered at the top of his lungs, hoping the bluff would work because he wasn't about to shoot anybody in the back.

Snapping branches momentarily distracted him. He pivoted. Thought he heard an engine rev in the distance. There might still be time to at least track the thief or thieves, even if he wasn't fast enough to catch up on foot.

He raced for the porch and met Maggie face-to-face as she jerked open the door.

Her eyes were wide. Filled with fright. She zeroed in on the gun in his hand. "What happened?"

"Somebody was raiding your meds. Call the sheriff and tell him I'm in pursuit."

"You're leaving us?"

"Harlan will be out ASAP—this is no minor incident. If I don't go now the snow will cover the tracks and we'll lose our chance."

There was little doubt Maggie didn't want him to go. But he had to. Not only was it his job to take care of crime in the wilderness, but this was the best opportunity they'd had to identify the person or persons who had been endangering her.

Flint could tell when she shifted mind-sets to embrace his opinion, even before she spoke.

"Okay. Go. I'll lock the doors and call for help. Which way are you headed?"

"East, from the sound of it. I think I heard a vehicle start after the guy ran." He ducked to place a quick kiss on her flushed cheek. "Make that call."

Snow kept falling. So did temperatures. It was almost an hour before Harlan pulled up in Maggie's yard.

She was so frantic she threw open the door and began to shout before he got all the way to the porch. "Where have you been? It's pitch-dark out there and Flint's all alone. You have to find him. Help him. I'd have gone, but Mark's asleep and I couldn't leave."

The portly sheriff stopped and shook himself like a damp dog before entering the house. "Now, now. Let's take a minute to talk about this," he drawled.

"Talk is useless. Flint is out there chasing

crooks, and he hasn't called or anything. You need to organize a search party and go after him."

Shrugging out of his coat, he hung it on a chair and splayed his icy fingers in front of her fire. "Can't send anybody out there even if I could spare 'em, and I can't. We've got multiple wrecks on the roads thanks to this storm," Harlan said. "I shook loose to check on you, but everybody else is tied up. Your game warden will have to look after himself. Besides, if I add more men to the confusion before it stops snowing, we'll have a worse mess."

Maggie wanted desperately to argue her point but had no appropriate words. The older man was right.

"Have you tried to call Flint?" the sheriff asked.

She shook her head. "No. I was afraid, if he was sneaking up on somebody, the ringing of his cell would give him away."

"Well, maybe. It's up to you. Course, if I was him I'd have my phone set on silent."

"That's right!" She snatched up her own phone and punched his preset number. "It's ringing."

Harlan was rubbing his hands together, looking pleased.

"Hey," she heard, followed by crackling that sounded like cellophane being crumpled.

"Flint? Where are you?"

"Halfway up Ni...ge," he said.

"You're breaking up. Can you get to a higher place so the signal is stronger?"

This time, his "No" was very clear. And hoarse.

"Are you on your way back?" Maggie held her breath, waiting. The phone was silent.

"Flint!" she shouted. "Talk to me."

"Trap," he said, followed by what sounded like his teeth chattering.

"They *trapped* you?" Maggie covered the speaker on her phone to tell the sheriff, "He's trapped."

Moments later there was more static. Amid the background noise she heard, "Bear," or thought she did, and held up her hand.

"You're in a *bear* trap?" Maggie could barely breathe, barely form the words. "Where?"

This time she was sure she heard the word *mile*. Putting his previous attempts together, she guessed, "Nine Mile Ridge? Are you near where we used to go for picnics in the summer?"

"Ye—s."

"All right. Stay put. Somebody will be there soon." She looked to the sheriff. "I know where he is. You have to hurry. If I understood him right and he's stepped in a real bear trap, his leg is broken for sure."

Harlan shook his head, his tone somber. "Can't do it, girl. Much as I'd like to, I know I'd never make it, and all my other men are working accidents. What about Game and Fish? Want me to try to get ahold of them?"

"Yes!" She was bouncing on her toes, barely able to stand in one place.

As she listened to the sheriff speaking to Flint's office, she watched him. His expression was not promising. Nor were his results. "They say they'll kick some men loose in maybe an hour or so, but they're as busy as my officers are because of the storm. Civilian rescues come first. I'm sorry."

"No. No, no, no," Maggie insisted. "I'm not leaving Flint out there to freeze or bleed to death while we sit on our hands and wait."

She donned heavy socks, then boots, then the warmest jacket she owned layered with a sweater, scarf and knit hat. The cell phone went into her jeans pocket before she pulled on thick gloves.

"You can't go out there," Harlan said firmly. "I'd rather give it a try than let you risk your life on a fool's errand. You've got a child to think of."

"I *am* thinking of him." Maggie was adamant. "I know every inch of these woods. It would take me longer to tell you where to look than it will for me to hike up there on my own. You stay here with Mark. I'll phone you as soon as I find Flint."

"If you find him."

"Oh, I'll find him," she said. "And bring him back with me, one way or another."

FIFTEEN

Cold seeped into Flint's bones and dulled more and more of the excruciating pain. He would have been able to free himself if he hadn't fallen backward and ended up practically dangling from a steel cable by his ankle. Snow had masked the snare trap as well as the fallen limbs near it, and he was tangled so badly he'd been unable to extricate himself.

Although he had managed to prop a shoulder against a tree stump to keep blood from rushing to his brain, he was only half sitting up. Originally, he'd spent his time trying to figure out how to free himself. Now he was past that, accepting of his fate to the point where he'd have been concerned if he hadn't been so sleepy.

The more soporific he grew, the more his mind drifted and came up with options he'd never have considered under normal circumstances. Shoot the thin steel wire? Shoot the tree it was anchored to? he wondered, before realizing how far from normal good sense he'd wandered. That helped snap him out of his stupor temporarily.

Deciding to act on the yearning to once again hear Maggie's voice, he reached for his phone—and found it buried in a drift beside him. Not only was the instrument wet now, but ice crystals had had time to form on the screen.

Flint cradled the useless phone. "Ah, Maggie, I did try," he whispered through cracking lips. "It was for you. All for you. I hope you know that."

Closing his eyes, he recalled his long-ago decision to leave Serenity. It wasn't only her brothers' aggression that had convinced him to go away. It was knowing that if they married and remained there, the way Maggie wanted, they'd be constantly bombarded by negative concepts. What chance would their marriage have had then?

And now? Flint tried to draw a deep breath, but the icy air felt like needles in his throat and lungs. He'd done his best to protect her, to figure out who was threatening her. That was why he'd taken the chance of venturing out in the storm.

He cast his eyes toward the gray sky and blinked against the falling snow. "Where are You, Lord?" he asked prayerfully. "I thought you'd sent me to help Maggie, so how come I'm stuck here freezing to death?"

Even in his altered state of understanding, he

realized he'd failed to be thankful for all he'd been given. He pictured his beautiful little boy, and tears froze on his lashes. "Take care of them," Flint prayed. "Please, God. Thank You for the time I did have, for getting to meet Mark and see Maggie again. Forgive me for all my mistakes and let them know I did my best."

As he fell silent he heard a branch crack. Then another. Given the way sound traveled in the forest, the noises could have come from anywhere.

His gun lay on his lap. It took both hands to pick it up and even then he wasn't sure he could make his gloved fingers bend enough to pull the trigger if he had to defend himself.

"Strength, Father. Please," he said through chattering teeth. Then he waited.

Maggie had been wise enough to pick up a flashlight and a small blue tarp on her way out of the compound. She had no intention of spending the night in the woods, but it never hurt to be prepared, just in case.

Following Flint's tracks was impossible given the recent snowfall. If he hadn't told her where to look for him, she wouldn't have ventured out at all. The sheriff was right about it being foolhardy—unless a person had the advantages she possessed. Not only did she know the woods, probably better than just about anybody, but she remembered the place where she and Flint had often shared a picnic lunch. It wasn't far. Going there would put her in the right vicinity. After that, she'd have to rely on intuition.

No. On prayer, Maggie reminded herself. "A sinking-ship, leaking-lifeboat kind of prayer." She almost smiled behind the scarf covering the lower half of her face. That might be a silly way of expressing it, but the concept was valid. Some of her most fervent prayers had come from situations she'd thought were impossible to overcome.

"Father," she said, steadily plodding ahead, "I'm sorry for being so testy with Flint. Please guide me? Help me to help him?"

I have to find him, she added silently. *I can't leave him out here, alone and hurt.*

Topping a ridge, she removed one glove and pulled out her phone. No service. There should have been a strong signal, meaning the cell towers were probably coated with ice and snow already.

She wanted to cry. To fall to her knees and sob. But she didn't. She stuffed the phone back in her pocket, slipped her glove back on before her fingers got too cold and kept moving.

As she hiked, her heart and mind kept calling out to her heavenly Father. And every time she felt a new surge of power and conviction she added, "Thank You, Jesus."

It was all that kept her going.

* * *

Flint's vision blurred, his eyelids drooping repeatedly. He snapped them open for the umpteenth time. He must not sleep. Must not…

Something popped and cracked nearby, jarring him back to more clarity. Was the cold affecting the trees or was he hearing something else? He tensed, hoping he'd be able to lift his handgun in case the noise came from an enemy rather than a rescuer or a natural source. Although he had no idea how much time had passed, he assumed there would be a team on his trail by now, perhaps even Wallace and Samson. At this point he didn't care how much they teased him for stepping in a snare and getting jerked off his feet as long as they packed him out of this icebox.

When he tried to move, he discovered that the back of his jacket had frozen to the side of the stump. Ripping it loose caused his ankle to twist farther and he was unable to stifle a groan.

Silence ensued. Flint gritted his teeth, waiting for the throbbing in his foot and leg to subside.

Something else drifted to him. Was he hallucinating? Had someone called his name? He was about to attribute the faint sound to wishful thinking when he heard it again.

"Here! Over here!" He thought he was shouting, but his raspy cry was almost lost on the wind, soaked up by the snow blanket. He tried again. "Here!"

No one answered.

Flint waited as long as he could, then sagged back. His mind was surely playing tricks on him, which was one of the signs that his body was nearly through fighting. "Father, tell Maggie..." he began before complete defeat overtook him and his eyes closed.

Excited, relieved and so overcome she could hardly speak, Maggie fell to her knees beside Flint and heard him mumbling her name. "I'm here."

The green eyes opened and focused on her. "Ummm. Dreaming," Flint murmured.

"No, you're not dreaming," she assured him. "I'm really here. I found you."

"Thank G-God."

"I know. I already have. It's amazing." The more she talked to him, the more he seemed to rally. She'd lowered her scarf to speak and was shining the beam of the flashlight on her face so he could see her smile. "I'm so glad to see you. Why did you say you were caught in a bear trap?"

"Lousy connection. I said *snare*."

"You have no idea what a relief that is. I figured you were out here about to loose a foot."

"Still might. Tangled. Get men. H-help me up."

"That could take a while," Maggie said with an arch of her eyebrows under the rim of her knit hat. "There weren't any others available when I talked to you on the phone. Every able-bodied soul is out rescuing civilians. Professionals are supposed to be able to take care of themselves."

"Call for help?" he managed.

She could tell speaking was a struggle for him. "No cell service out here. I already tried. The towers must have iced over."

Backing off, she played the flashlight beam over him and assessed his situation. "I think I can release you. Is your ankle broken?"

"Not sure," Flint said. He shook himself and slapped his own face with an icy glove. "Did you just say you came alone?"

"It was me or nobody. The sheriff was barely able to make it from his car to the porch."

"What were you thinking?"

"That I'd lose you if I didn't do something," she answered, glad to note anger in his tone because that would increase his circulation and actually help. "So I did something. I came after you."

"M-Mark?"

"Is home in bed while Harlan keeps the fire going and probably eats me out of house and home." Maggie tried another smile despite Flint's evident ire.

"H-how do you propose to get me there?"

"Good question. I suppose we could make camp and wait out the storm, but you didn't look so good when I first got here. I think I'd best figure out a way to get you to civilization."

"Leave me. Go back to our son. I don't want him to lose us both."

"That's the hypothermia talking." Pulling out the small blue tarp, she unfolded it and laid it over him. "I'm going to try to pull this wire down first." She put all her weight on the trap cable. Her icy gloves kept slipping. "Okay. Plan B. I'll lift you up so you can help me."

"Lift me?" Flint tried to laugh and coughed instead.

"Yes, lift you. I buck bales of hay by myself all the time." She eyed the tangle of branches where he'd landed. "How did you get yourself into such a mess?"

"Fell backward," he rasped. "Upside down."

She started to break away the thinner limbs and cast them aside. "The trapper probably set his loop there because large game would naturally avoid the deadfalls. You did the same. Good thing that whoever you were chasing in the first place didn't double back and find you like this."

"Yeah. If they had I'd really be a goner." Flint had hunkered down beneath the tarp, only flinching when she bumped his leg. "Stupid."

"What? You, me or the tree snag?" Now that

she'd located him, Maggie's spirits were so high she had to morph her joy into silliness or lose control.

"Jokes?"

She could tell he was far from entertained at the moment. "Sorry. I'm so glad to see you I don't know what to do with myself. It's jokes or hysteria. You choose."

"Wh-whatever gets me out of this mess," Flint said.

Tugging on bent branches, she managed to snap one of the largest limbs, tumbling backward with a shriek as it broke.

"Good one," Flint said wryly. "You okay?" He'd tucked all but his eyes under the tarp and seemed to be recovering, much to her relief.

Maggie struggled to her feet, brushed off clinging snow and approached again to check the scene with her light. "I think that did it. I'm going to get behind you, lift and push. As soon as you're standing, try to grab the snare and hang on."

Although she did her best to be gentle, he still made a guttural noise that carried through the silent night.

"Sorry." She was breathless, leaning into him with her full weight. "For once I wish I was as big as Harlan."

"Me, too," Flint said. "Aaaah."

From behind him Maggie couldn't see what

he was doing, but the relief from the back pressure told her enough. She struggled out of the depression, over the remaining broken branches, and jumped to wrap her hands above his.

"It's looser," she gasped. "Can you work your boot out?"

"I'm trying."

She lost her grip on the thin wire cable and fell.

"You try while I pull down," Flint ordered.

This had to work. It had to. The wire had left an indentation in his leather boot, so no telling how badly it might have squeezed his ankle. If too much circulation was cut off for too long, he could eventually lose his foot. She'd seen it happen to animals.

"I don't want to hurt you."

"Do it! Pull the heel."

So Maggie did. And felt his pain all the way to her own toes.

When Flint was free they both collapsed in the snow, breathless.

Success gave her hope and made her a bit giddy. "Well, that was fun. What would you like to do next?"

"Stand," he said, gritting his teeth. "I'm afraid you'll have to help me again. I'm back in that low spot."

"Excuses, excuses, excuses," she gibed. "Okay.

Take my hand this time." A mighty tug was almost enough to pull her into the hole on top of him.

She stepped back. "Well, that's not going to work. Now that you can turn over, how about rolling out?"

"I'll try. My foot's numb. Look around for something I can use like a cane."

"Gotcha."

Maggie found a strong limb and prayed while she watched Flint struggle. On his third try he was able to turn enough to crawl to flatter ground. From there he pulled himself up on a stalwart oak. His face was ashen again and he was panting, but at least he was up.

Her muscles were also tied in knots. She rolled her shoulders and handed him the strong staff to lean on. "Whew. I'm exhausted."

"Makes two of us. Grab the tarp so we'll have shelter in case we don't make it all the way back."

"We'll make it," Maggie promised. "We got this far. We can't quit now."

Before they tried to walk together, Flint practiced by taking a few faltering steps, then told her to take up a supportive position on his injured side. As long as he didn't twist his ankle or put his full weight on it, the pain wasn't too severe. But the going was slow.

"How are you holding up?" he asked Maggie, wondering how much time had actually passed.

"I'm okay."

"We could stop and rest. How much farther is it?"

"I've kind of lost track," Maggie admitted. "I thought you were paying attention. You've got the flashlight."

"Yeah. Does it look dimmer to you?"

"I hadn't noticed."

But he had. And chances were they'd run out of battery power before they reached her house. There were game trails in this area, though. If they could intersect one of those...

Flint sniffed the icy air. "Wait. Do you smell smoke?"

"Yes!"

He switched off the light and waited for his eyes to adjust. "Which way?"

Maggie pointed. "There. To the right. I think that's my place!"

Peering through the trees and blowing snow, he thought he noticed a flickering yellow spot. It could be coming from her window. Or someone else's. At this point they couldn't be picky.

Flint felt a surge of elation coupled with a last burst of energy. They were going to make it.

She lagged. "Wait. What if that's not my house? What if it's a fire set to draw us in and trap us?"

"Either way we'll get warmed up. After that

we can worry about danger. Or would you prefer to freeze to death out here?"

"Of course not. I just thought—"

"That *you* should decide how the Lord saves us?" Flint chuckled wryly. "I don't know about you, but I've been praying ever since I left to chase the thief."

"So have I. Sort of. Mostly I was asking for help finding you."

He leaned into the wind and urged her along. "Which you did. But it won't do either of us a bit of good if we don't make it to shelter. And I don't mean that little makeshift tent you brought along."

"Oh, fine. Now you're complaining about my preparations. I'm surprised you didn't berate me for not bringing wire cutters."

He laughed again, balanced with the staff and hugged her close with his free arm. "Not really, honey. I'm just glad you're here to tease." Flint sobered. "Tonight could have ended very differently."

"I don't think so." He thought he heard a catch in her voice as she continued with "I wasn't about to give up on you again. Once was plenty."

SIXTEEN

Maggie had never seen a more welcome sight. She began to shout as soon as they broke out of the forest and entered the clearing by her house. "Harlan. Help! Help us."

They were struggling up the porch steps before the sheriff opened the door. "Mercy sakes."

He relieved Maggie of her burden and dragged Flint through the door, not letting him go until they were all warming in front of a blazing fire.

She recovered her voice first. "Everybody else is still out on other calls?"

"Yes. There's a bunch of lost kids out by the cell tower in Horseshoe and another emergency rescue at the Strawberry River. Snow makes people do crazy things."

Maggie huffed and stared pointedly at Flint. "I can vouch for that."

Still standing, Harlan was assessing them. "Will you two be okay if I skedaddle? They need me out there to coordinate another team of my people. I shouldn't have stayed away as long as I did."

"Thanks for looking after Mark," she said. "I'm okay if Flint is. He wasn't stuck in a bear trap like I thought, but he does have a sore ankle."

"I'll be fine. You go, Sheriff," Flint assured him. "It's probably just a sprain."

"If you're sure. I hate to leave unless you're sure you can defend yourselves."

Maggie had to smile when Flint paraphrased something she'd often heard from her own mother. "If it ain't bleedin', I ain't hurt bad."

Harlan nodded and pulled on his heavy jacket. "I'll send somebody later to check on you folks or swing by myself. If this snow keeps up it may be a while, though."

"We'll be fine," Maggie said. "I'm well stocked for emergencies." Her grin widened. "And I know the warden will behave because he's stove in."

Chuckling, the older man bid them a quick goodbye and left. When Maggie looked back at Flint he was frowning. "What?"

"You made it sound as if you only trust me because I'm hurt."

She had to laugh. "Don't take yourself so seriously, Crawford. After all we've just been through, we should both be so thankful we're dancing around the room."

"Pardon me if I take a rain check on that," he

grumbled. With a grimace he lifted his booted foot to rest on the raised stone hearth while he shrugged out of his damp coat.

"It was a figure of speech," Maggie insisted. "You get comfortable and dry out. I'm going to go make coffee and hot soup to warm our insides, too."

Halfway out of the room she hesitated. "You are all right, aren't you? I mean, if you thought you had frostbite you'd have told Harlan and gone with him for treatment, wouldn't you?"

"Yeah, sure."

"You don't sound convincing."

"Probably because I haven't taken my boot off and looked yet, and my foot feels like pins and needles. Want to give me a hand?"

She was sorely tempted to applaud and give him a hand that way before helping with his boot, but she managed to restrain the urge to be so silly. If she let herself think too deeply about what had happened and acknowledge the dire possibilities they'd avoided, she was afraid she might weep.

Flint must have sensed her fluctuating mood, because he frowned at her and said, "Just help me ease it out, please. Before my foot gets warmer and starts to swell and we have to cut a good boot. And no jokes. I'm not up for that right now."

"Okay, okay." Maggie rejoined him. "Ready?"

"No, but the only way I'm going to be able to assess the damage is to look, so I guess I'd better *get* ready."

"I'll go slowly. Tell me if it hurts too much."

"It already hurts too much," Flint said dryly. "Go ahead. Pull."

She'd barely touched the boot when she heard his sharp intake of breath. "Sorry."

"It's okay. Keep going."

From the place where the hallway opened into the living room, they heard a faint "Mama?"

"Uh-oh. We woke Mark," she said.

"Sounds like it." Flint looked over at his son. The child was rubbing sleep from his eyes while his dog panted beside him. "Hi, buddy. You should be in bed."

"What happened?" Padding closer, the boy was clearly concerned.

"The warden hurt his ankle," Maggie explained. "Why don't you go get me a clean towel to dry his foot with when I get his boot off?"

The green eyes widened. "Is he bleeding like Wolfie did?"

"No, honey. Just very cold."

"Okay." Mark spun and disappeared back into the hall. When he returned he was dragging his favorite blue blanket. He only hesitated a second before offering it to his father.

"Better take it," Maggie told Flint. "He loves

that ratty old thing like a best friend. It's really special for him to loan it to you."

Flint smiled at Mark and said, "Thanks. Why don't you sit on my lap so we can share it?"

"Okay."

While they were busy interacting and she knew Flint wouldn't want to express pain, she slowly inched his boot farther and farther. Though he did flinch a couple of times, he withstood the soreness well.

"Got it," Maggie said proudly. She set the soggy boot aside and started to remove his sock. Judging by the way he was gritting his teeth again, this hurt. A lot.

"Why don't you go get Mommy that dry towel now?" Maggie said to Mark. The five-year-old didn't look pleased to have to leave the room, but he obeyed.

Flint's eyes were damp and his cheeks flushed again. "Hurry up and finish torturing me, will you? I don't want my son to think I'm a wimp."

"Never," Maggie assured him. "You're feeling the injury from the trap and the cold together. It's bound to be a nasty combination."

"That's onc way to put it."

She dropped the wet sock on the hearth and began to gently examine his foot and ankle. There was some light bruising around the Achilles tendon and across the top of the arch, but it really didn't look too bad. Nevertheless, after she had checked the foot for visible injuries, she continued to hold and caress it. "You're freezing."

"You will be, too, if you don't stop touching me."

"Is that an objection?" she asked, realizing she was acting as much from her own desires as from a need to impart comfort.

"Yes," Flint said gruffly. He pulled his foot from her grasp and propped it across his knee so he could look for himself. "Maybe a few pulled tendons or ligaments, but I don't think it's broken," he announced, sounding relieved.

"Good. I'll go make that coffee and soup now."

"You do that." Mark had returned and was handing a clean white towel to Flint. "Make it hot chocolate for me, please. And one for my helpful friend." As he spoke he pulled Mark's tattered blanket closer around his shoulders and propped his injured foot on the folded towel to pad the heel and let his flesh warm slowly by the fire.

Maggie was thankful for many things as she left them. If Flint had gotten much colder, he'd have had to bring the foot back to life via cold water baths. Since he wasn't asking for that treatment, chances were good that he didn't think he had frostbite. Hypothermia was enough. More than enough. If she had not decided to go after him…

The thought of his suffering and dying out there was so dreadful she could hardly breathe.

She couldn't see past the tears in her eyes until they began to course down her cheeks. Stifling sobs, she covered her mouth with both hands.

Thank God, literally, that she hadn't broken down like this in front of Flint. It would have been far too revealing. He didn't even want her to rub circulation back into his injured foot. What would he have to say if she hugged him the way she yearned to and cried all over his wrinkled Sunday shirt?

Maggie grabbed a dish towel, pressed it against her face to absorb any noise and sobbed her heart out.

Then she pulled herself together, brewed coffee and hot cocoa and stirred up a pot of chicken noodle soup. If anyone asked about her reddened eyes, she'd blame the cold weather she'd recently been exposed to. That was plausible as well as a true contributing factor.

Nobody, especially not Flint Crawford, was going to guess how much she still loved him. Later, when and if life settled down to halfway normal, she might admit her burgeoning feelings. But it had to be done right. Calmly and sensibly, not in the same frenetic manner as years before.

In retrospect, she realized the blame was as much hers as his. They had both made irrational demands, sticking to them even when it was plain that doing so doomed their romance. If that mistake had taught her nothing else, it had demonstrated how give-and-take was a crucial part of any relationship.

That, and heartfelt prayer. Nothing in life went nearly as well if she forgot to pray about it, particularly if she waited, as usual, until she was already in deep trouble.

She glanced toward the living room. "Yeah, like now."

A dull pulsing in Flint's foot was uncomfortable, but he wasn't complaining. No, sirree. Feeling a heartbeat meant the tiny blood vessels were still functioning. The more they throbbed, the more positive he was that he was going to be fine. Given his earlier doubts, he welcomed the painful assurance.

Maggie had carried their son off to bed, then brought extra blankets for him and spread them on the sofa. She'd lingered by the fireplace, giving him the notion that she wanted to talk, yet had said very little. Mostly, she seemed exhausted.

That was no surprise. How she'd managed to find him, free him and get him back there all by herself was amazing.

"In case I forgot to mention it, thanks for coming after me," Flint said amiably.

"You're welcome."

"It was very brave."

"Thanks."

"And really, really dumb."

That got her attention. "I beg your pardon?"

"Mark. How could you take a risk like that when you know he depends on you?"

"He deserves a father, too. I knew where you were and how to reach you. What's risky about that?"

Flint rolled his eyes. "Oh, please. You were not only alone and out of touch with anybody, but you were unarmed." A furtive look from Maggie made him ask, "You didn't have a gun, did you?"

"No. You'd locked up my bullets. I figured, once I got to you, if there was a need I could use your handgun."

"Did we bring it back with us? I remember holding it and wondering if I could make my fingers bend enough to pull the trigger, but I don't remember picking it up."

"You didn't. I did. It's on top of the fridge," she said smugly. "You were pretty out of it."

Flint knew he owed her plenty, probably his life, but it still galled to have to admit it. "Guess so." The arch of her eyebrows amused him and he chuckled. "What? You think I don't really appreciate what you did? Well, I do. I just wish you'd found a saner way to accomplish it."

"That would have been easier if you hadn't decided to chase a thief in the middle of a snow-storm."

"You do have a point there." Taking a deep

breath and noting that his throat felt soothed after the hot liquids, Flint leaned back against the pillow Maggie had propped on one armrest of the sofa. Finally, he said, "It was not my finest hour."

"So why did you do it?"

Although he was pretty sure he knew why, he chose to avoid a direct answer. "Adrenaline, maybe. And wanting to end all the harassment. If we could be sure exactly who was behind the shootings and vandalism and break-ins, it would be a lot easier to catch and punish them."

"I thought you were positive it was Elwood's doing."

"His or the Dodds'. Elwood's slippery. We've repeatedly sent men to all three of the cabins he's been known to occupy in the past and found no sign of him. That means either he's on the run and trying to keep from being caught, as usual, or he's not around at all."

"Which do you think it is?" Maggie asked, stifling a yawn.

"Most of the clues seem to fit his style, but some things don't add up. Like the truck that hit you. There's nothing matching that description registered to any of the Witherspoons, and both Dodds drive cars."

Watching her, Flint glimpsed a flash of insight that came and went in moments. Propped on one elbow, he pinned her with his gaze. "You just had an idea. I can tell."

She shook her head and set her jaw.

"Come on. Spill it. We need to work together on this whether you want to or not."

"I never said I didn't want to," she insisted. "Call it self-preservation. The last time I brought this up you nearly bit my head off."

"No way." Slumping back against the pillow, he refused to consider what he now suspected was on her mind. "There are no Crawfords left around here but Bess, Ira and me, so you can forget blaming us."

"You haven't overlooked some distant cousin or somebody like that?"

"No. I actually questioned Bess, which made me feel terrible, by the way, and she confirmed it. We know about every Crawford in the county and beyond. Too many of them met sad fates, much like my mother and hers before her. That's why Ira won't even take an aspirin for a head-ache. He's made up his mind that all drugs are poison, even prescription ones."

"Doesn't he take something for his dementia?"

"Not that I'm aware of." Flint knew where she was going with her query and didn't like it one bit. "All that's done is make the disease progress faster. I told you. He's unable to function the way he used to. It's sad but true, so you can cross him off your suspect list."

"Okay." Maggie yawned. "If you have everything you need, I guess I'll see you in the morning, then."

"I'm good. I'll be sure to keep the fire going."

"It's banked," she countered. "You shouldn't have to do much before morning. We're halfway through the night already." Another yawn.

Flint mirrored her. "Yeah. Harlan will probably be back here asking for pancakes in a couple of hours. We'd better get some sleep."

"Right. Good night."

Watching her leave, Flint realized how weary—and how wide-awake—he was. Being around Maggie stole his sleep and left him more confused by the minute. She was so brave she was scary. And yet he admired her courage. He just wished it didn't keep getting her into trouble—like when she'd testified on behalf of Abigail Dodd's sanity.

Lacing his fingers behind his head to cradle it, he readjusted his throbbing ankle. Maggie wasn't the only one who did foolish things. He'd gone into a snowstorm dressed for church, for crying out loud, so there was no way he could fault only her. If he hadn't grabbed his heavy work jacket on his way out, he probably wouldn't be alive to complain about anything.

Flint's thoughts spun through his mind like an Arkansas tornado, touching ground here and there and leaving a path of destruction. And, like the aftermath of a real tornado, he could tell it was going to be necessary to wait for the dust to settle before trying to sort out the rubble. To find the worthwhile things. To salvage the unbroken or repair what was left and move on.

He knew what he wanted to find. He simply wasn't sure there would be enough left of his and Maggie's previous lives to restore and revive.

Closing his eyes, Flint thought of his reaction when she'd become the answer to his prayers for rescue mere hours before. Instead of thanking God for sending help, he'd argued that Maggie was the wrong person.

With a sigh he finally admitted what he'd known all along. Like it or not, Maggie was decidedly the *right* person, in more ways than one.

Almost asleep, he thought he heard something. Outside? Inside? Flint tensed. Strained to listen.

Outside. Definitely outside. What had Maggie said she'd done with his handgun? He knew she would have made sure it was out of Mark's reach, but where had she stashed it? *That's right. Atop the refrigerator!*

Starting to swing his legs over the side of the couch and sit up, Flint was startled by a loud pounding on the door. He jumped. Bumped his foot. Sent fire and ice shooting up his leg. And cried out in pain.

SEVENTEEN

Maggie was running before she was fully awake. She swung around the corner into the living room and saw the agony on Flint's face. "What happened?"

"I moved too fast. Where's my gun?"

The pounding continued. "I'll get it. Stay there."

"Like I'd *go* someplace?" Flint grumbled.

"I heard that." She returned with the handgun carefully pointed away from him, her finger nowhere near the trigger.

"It's a wonder you heard anything over that banging." He was nearly shouting.

"Who is it?" she asked.

"I have no idea. They didn't bother to announce themselves." Flint pushed to his feet, using the back of the sofa for support, and aimed at the door. "Who's there?"

Silence followed. Maggie couldn't stand not knowing, so she started forward.

"Wait," Flint ordered. "Stay back."

"Don't be silly. If they were up to no good, they wouldn't knock."

"They might." Flint raised his voice again. "Tell us who you are or go away."

"It's me," a youthful voice replied.

Maggie recognized it immediately and jerked open the door. "Robbie. What's wrong?"

Instead of answering, he plunged through the opening and slammed the heavy door behind him. "They're coming."

"Who's coming?" Flint demanded.

Maggie didn't like the way he kept his gun aimed at the teenager, so she gently pushed the barrel aside. "You don't have to worry about Robbie. It's the others who're the problem."

"That's what I'm trying to tell you," Robbie blurted. "Papaw's taken a notion that Warden Crawford's moved in with you and he's comin' here to shoot him."

"Why?" She was astounded.

"'Cause he's plumb crazy, that's why," the youth said, still breathless. "He keeps callin' you Elizabeth and sayin' he's gonna rescue you."

It took Maggie a moment to realize that *Bess* was a shorter version of that name. Her gaze shot to Flint. His eyes were narrowed, his brow creased, his jaw muscles clenching. Clearly, he had come to the same conclusion.

"How did you get over here?" Flint asked.

"Walked," Robbie said. "That's the only reason I was able to beat 'em. Papaw Elwood's slow, particularly in the snow."

Maggie went to the window and peered out. "Looks like it's still coming down."

In the reflection on the glass she saw Flint testing his ankle and grimacing as he took several steps. She turned to face him. "What're we going to do?"

"Make a stand," Flint said flatly. He eyed the teenager. "Which side are you on, son?"

"Yours."

Maggie could tell Flint wasn't convinced. She wasn't, either. It was one thing to fight with a stranger and quite another to take on a relative, particularly one who had helped raise you.

"Are you sure?" she asked Robbie. "You can still make a run for it and they'll never know you came here to warn us."

He shook his head adamantly. "I'm stayin'. I never did abide what Papaw was doin'. My brothers, either. I can't run off and let 'em hurt somebody, not even a Crawford."

That made Flint snort. "Since you put it that way, what're you going to use for a weapon?"

"Left my shotgun on the porch," Robbie said, blushing and staring at the handgun. "I figured if I busted in here carrying, you'd blow me away."

"Could have happened," Flint said flatly.

Maggie hoped he was exaggerating, since she

wasn't in favor of anybody getting killed, yet how could they avoid Elwood's pending attack? "Can we use your AGFC truck to get away?" she asked Flint.

"It's risky, but it might work," he replied before looking at Robbie. "Providing nobody let the air out again. How much time do you think we have?"

"No tellin'. I left while they was gettin' ready, but I don't think they were far behind."

"Okay. Go get your shotgun and check my truck while you're out there. If it looks okay we'll load up and make a run for it."

The young man had barely left the house when he was back, wild-eyed and trembling. "Too late. They're here. I saw Luke. Can't tell where Papaw is, but he's gotta be out there."

As Maggie's eyes met Flint's she saw both determination and sorrow. He hobbled toward her. "Okay. You go into the bedroom with the boy and hide. Both of you. Take your cell phone with you and keep trying to call the sheriff, just in case the phones start working."

"I don't want—"

"I know. I don't want to leave you, either, but we can't always have what we want."

The double meaning in his words was not lost on her. He might as well have been referring to their parting six years ago.

"All right. I'll be in the closet with Mark and

Wolfie. It's where I put them before, so they're less likely to panic this time."

"And the dog will defend you?" Flint asked.

"I'm sure he will." Maggie wasn't positive, but there was no way she was going to saddle Flint with more worry. Her best defense was probably going to be Elwood's belief that she was his long-lost betrothed.

She spun on her heels and ran for Mark's bedroom. The child was sitting up in bed, keeping a tight grip on the dog's collar. His voice was shaky. "What's wrong?"

"We need to go into your camping place again," Maggie said.

"Why?"

"Because I said so." She had no time for arguments or explanations. Catching the small child around his waist, she called the dog to follow and tucked them all in the closet in the dark. Thankfully, the extra bedding was still on the floor so they'd be warm enough, as if a panting dog wasn't enough radiant heat.

"This time, we're going to pretend we're invisible," she whispered, ruing the fear tingeing her voice as she pulled one of the blankets over them all and embraced her frightened little boy.

Mark was the only reason she'd been able to force herself to leave Flint. A mother's love was strong. So was that which had survived between her and Flint in spite of everything and was now tearing her heart into tiny pieces and leaving her despondent.

There was absolutely nothing else she could do besides exactly what she was already doing. When she'd ventured into the snowstorm to find Flint, she knew where she was going and how to get there successfully. Now she had no idea what was happening. Furthermore, she was far too distressed to come up with any kind of prayer, no matter how badly she wanted to.

The love of her life was about to lay his own life on the line for hers. And for their child's. At that moment, she could not have loved Flint more.

Or feared more for his survival.

Hearing a moderate knock on the door, Flint motioned Robbie aside and called, "Who's there?"

When there was no answer he took a step closer and raised his voice. "I said, who—"

Gunfire cut him off. He dove for cover, hoping and praying that the sound of shooting wouldn't draw Maggie out of hiding.

He'd subconsciously counted the number of shots, confused about the capacity of whatever firearm Elwood was using until he noticed the uneven splintering on the inside of the wooden door. The old man was evidently firing at least two different calibers simultaneously, or the younger ones were also shooting. Hopefully, they'd soon have to stop to reload.

"Go stand guard at the back." Flint gestured at Robbie. "Don't let anybody sneak up behind me."

The youth crab-walked across the littered floor, dragging his shotgun, and disappeared in the dark.

If Flint had had time, he might have doused the glowing fireplace to further darken the room, but it was too late for that. They already knew he was in there. And if they managed to breach the door, he'd have only one chance, one option. He'd have to take out whoever came at him firing.

Maggie's kin. The Witherspoon who, if legends and rumors were to be believed, had lost everything to his grandfather Ira and had eventually also lost his mind.

Both old men were suffering for their past deeds and attitudes, weren't they? Their spirits had dwelt on the feud for so long it had cost them a lot more than it would have if they had simply forgiven each other for the animosity that had grown out of their words and deeds. How many other lives had their anger ruined? How many unnecessary tears had been shed?

Sounds of clicking came from outside. Elwood, or whoever was on the porch, had just snapped the cylinder back into a revolver. When he didn't immediately begin firing, Flint limped forward. His hand was on the doorknob when he heard a shotgun action levering a live shell into the chamber.

He jerked his hand back and flattened his back to the adjoining wall. The knob and fittings around the lock disappeared in a shower of brass and lead and needle-sharp wood fragments.

Staggering back from the force, Flint put too much weight on his injured foot and fell. Rolled aside. Brought his sidearm into play as he heard a second shell being loaded.

Wild-eyed and raving, Elwood kicked open the broken door, raised a shotgun and pointed it at Flint.

A fraction of a second made the difference. They both fired, but the old man's aim was knocked high when he was hit squarely in the chest and propelled backward.

As Elwood collapsed in slow motion onto the snowy porch, Flint braced for the next attack.

It never came.

Maggie was trying to breathe. Her mouth was dry as cotton, her stomach roiling. She pulled Mark closer and closer until he objected. "Mama, too tight. Owie."

"I'm sorry, honey, I—"

Footsteps outside the closet door were soft, as if the person approaching was barefoot. Could it be? Did she dare hope? She choked back a sob.

"It's over, Maggie," a familiar voice called.

As the door started to open she leaped off the floor and threw herself at Flint, almost knocking him down again.

Clinging, she heard him say, "It was Elwood. I'm sorry," and she knew she should feel the same, but she didn't. Later she might be able to express genuine regret. Right now all that mattered was that they had survived. That Flint had come through it. That he was holding her. If anyone had managed to get her attention at that moment and ask what she wanted most, she would have said she already had it.

Mark tugged on her robe. "Mama? Mama?"

She felt Flint's hold on her loosen and she glanced down. "What, honey?"

"Can we come out, too?"

"Wait," Flint said. "I need to help Robbie straighten up a little in the front of the house."

"Is Elwood…?"

"On the porch, outside," Flint said. "Everybody else is fine. Even Robbie's brothers. They weren't nearly as bad-tempered once their grandfather was out of the picture."

She continued to cling to Flint. "Are you sure?"

"I'm sure. And very grateful," he replied. "I didn't want that poor kid to have to actually shoot anybody. That could scar him for life."

"Kind of like growing up in a town where half

the folks hate the other half and nobody is willing to let bygones be bygones?"

"Exactly." He gave her a squeeze and started to pull away. "I need to go make sure everything's okay."

Maggie held tightly to his waist. "Oh, no, you don't."

What she wanted to do was stand on tiptoe and kiss him, but she was afraid he might resist, so she said, "You scared me so badly I bit my lip, Flint Crawford. You need to kiss it and make it better."

"Really?" An eyebrow arched and green eyes pinned her in place, then drifted to her mouth. His thumb lightly skimmed her lower lip. "I don't see any damage."

She could hardly think, let alone speak, but she did manage to say, "I was terrified."

"Not as badly as I was," he countered, his voice rough yet tender. "Maybe *you* owe *me*."

The compassion and empathy in his expression provided all the assurance she needed. Loosening her hug, Maggie slipped both arms around his neck and tilted her head until their lips were nearly touching. It wasn't a surprise to feel that they were both trembling.

She closed her eyes. Flint brought his mouth to hers and lingered so gently it was like a whispered promise.

"It's been a long time," he said before kissing her again. And again.

"Too long," Maggie answered when he finally let her come up for air.

A sharp tug on her robe was followed by "I'm hungry."

Grinning, she eased away from Flint only slightly. "At least he didn't laugh at us."

"Yet," Flint added. He bent to pick up his son and carried him to the bedroom door before pressing the boy's face to his shoulder to keep him from seeing the aftereffects of the violence as they passed it.

"Stay in the kitchen and try to reach Harlan," Flint told Maggie. "Everything will be okay."

Her grin spread even wider. "It already is. Our family is still in one piece." She sobered slightly, feeling guilty. "I was so scared I couldn't even pray."

Flint cupped her cheek and lingered to caress it. "You don't have to perform a perfect spiritual rite to reach God," he said. "Prayers on a battlefield are just as compelling as the ones from church. Maybe more so."

"I'm sorry I never asked you about that. Was it terrible being sent overseas to fight?"

"Not as bad as it was tonight," he said with a telling sigh. "That crazy old fool left me no choice."

"I believe you." She was gazing lovingly into

the depths of his expressive green eyes and imagining a happy future. Finally.

Maggie shivered as Flint kissed her forehead and left her, wondering why she'd suddenly felt a twinge of lingering doubt. Perhaps it was because she was still recovering from the fright of being in the closet, where she could only imagine what was happening and therefore think the worst.

While Mark crawled onto a kitchen chair to wait for breakfast she rinsed and refilled the coffeemaker.

Knowing she'd need her biggest bowl in which to whip up enough pancake batter for the crowd in her living room, Maggie bent to retrieve it from a lower cabinet.

When she straightened, a flash of movement in the window over the sink was so startling she almost dropped the bowl. One blink and there was nothing there. Had there been? Of course not.

She shook off uneasiness, convinced her nerves were merely playing tricks on her. However, when she tried to pour Mark a glass of milk, her hands were trembling so badly she almost spilled it.

EIGHTEEN

Harlan or one of his deputies was yet to arrive, but at least the snow had stopped falling by the time Maggie had breakfast prepared.

Flint could tell that Robbie and his brothers were far from reconciled despite their outwardly calm attitudes. If he'd been by himself he'd have handcuffed the two older ones, but Maggie would have none of that.

"They're just disillusioned kids," she kept insisting.

"With rotten attitudes and weight-lifter bodies," Flint countered, speaking aside to her. "I'm not sure I'd win if they decided to jump me together."

She giggled. "I'd save you. We make quite a team."

"We do, don't we?"

"Uh-huh. If you're ready to brave eating with kids the size of linebackers for the Razorbacks, you can call them to the table."

"Sure. Just let me check my gun."

"Flint!"

He rolled his eyes as if they'd been joking. Maggie probably had been. He was dead serious. No way was he turning his back on those so-called kids, particularly since they'd been armed when they arrived with their grandfather. If one of them decided to avenge his death, Flint intended to be ready with an adequate defense.

The two older youths trailed Robbie into the kitchen and took the seats Flint pointed to. He wanted them both trapped between the table and a wall to limit their ability to act rashly. Or worse. He was no longer getting angry vibes from either of them. That could mean they were either biding their time or still in shock. It was no guarantee they might not decide to come after him later.

"You gonna read us our rights?" Luke asked.

Flint huffed. "Nope. Gonna feed you pancakes. Any objections?"

Even Robbie shook his head, although he was keeping a close eye on Will, the brother closest to him in age.

Giving the young men a chance to eat their fill, Flint made small talk about the weather and the food and living in a small town—anything he thought would distract them.

Luke eventually leaned back and patted his

stomach. "Real good, ma'am." His brothers agreed with profuse thanks.

"You're welcome," Maggie said. "Is everybody full or should I make another batch?"

Flint wasn't the only one who groaned. While everybody was smiling he said, "So, which one of you was driving the truck that shoved our pancake maker off the road?"

Three sets of hands were raised overhead, mimicking surrender. Luke and Will both shook their heads. "Not me."

"Me, neither."

"Are you blaming your grandpa?"

"Hey, cool it," Luke said, toning down his indignation as soon as Flint made serious eye contact. "I promise. We didn't do nothing like that. All's we did was make a few wolf sounds to scare her. It was all in fun."

"What about the fire? Which one of you is responsible for that? Robbie?"

He shook his head vigorously. "Not us. None of us. We didn't hear about it 'til after it was out."

"And the shooting?" Flint remained stony-faced, waiting for one of them to break.

It was Will who finally asked, "When?"

"More than once," Maggie offered, stopping when Flint gave her one of his steely stares.

"I can't speak for before, cause I don't know. We came along tonight when Papaw got to actin' all crazy, worse than usual, I mean." Luke said.

"He told us he wanted to go rescue some woman named Elizabeth and we had to come along. We all knew he was out of his head. I was afraid if we didn't come with him he'd turn around and shoot us dead on the spot."

Nods from the other boys showed agreement.

"What about poaching? You aren't planning on blaming that on Elwood, too, are you?"

"It was his idea," Robbie said quietly. "We just did as we was told."

"And sold the meat?"

"Well, yeah. Sometimes," Will replied. "Mostly we hunted deer in season, though."

"How many?" Flint didn't expect an honest answer. It was enough to see the boys blush and act uncomfortable.

Finally, Luke leaned forward with his forearms on the table and clasped his hands. "I'll take the fall for my brothers for breaking game laws," he said. "You can give me a lie detector test about any other shooting and you'll see it wasn't us. Honest."

Flint looked to Maggie. "What do you think?"

"I think they're telling the truth," she said with a sober nod before looking to Robbie. "What about Wolfie's paw? Are you the one who doctored him?"

The teenager suddenly found his napkin fascinating. "Yes, ma'am, Miz Maggie. I was afraid if I didn't tie him he'd follow me home and Papaw would shoot him. That's why I fired high to keep Crawford movin' out of that area, too."

"So you left Wolfie for me to find. I understand," she said. "Which one of you snuck into my house the other night? And who was rifling in the supply cabinet?"

Again, a chorus of "Not me" filled the room.

"What about the screen in Mark's room? Who took that off?"

Robbie interceded. "I wasn't with 'em all the time, but I can't see no reason for me or my brothers to bother you like that. The wolf calls was just for fun, like we said. Papaw told us we was supposed to just nettle you any time we got the chance, not hurt you bad or burn your place down. He said he wanted to stop folks like the warden from payin' so much attention to what went on in our neck of the woods, that's all."

"And tonight?" Flint leaned toward him across the table. "What was supposed to happen tonight?"

Tears filled the youngest teenager's eyes. "It started out to be a rescue. Honest. I figured there was likely to be fighting and such when Papaw grabbed a couple of his favorite guns, but I never thought he'd start shootin' wild like he did."

"What about you two?" Flint stared at Luke and Will.

"Us, either," Luke said. "But the closer we got,

the crazier he started talkin'. Pretty soon, it was like bein' with a stranger."

"Yeah," Will agreed. "I just held my fire and stood back. There was no tellin' what he'd do next, and I wanted to be able to duck behind a tree if it came to that."

"All right." Flint sighed. "Somebody will take your statements once we can get back to town. Be sure you tell them everything. And stick to the truth. It'll help you in the long run."

He rose, lifted Mark and held him at arm's length, facing away, to carry him to Maggie at the sink. "This has got to be the stickiest kid I have ever seen. Can you do something with him?"

"Not without a bath and clean clothes," she said, laughing lightly. "His feet are probably okay. Put him down and I'll walk him to the bathroom."

"Fine." Flint eyed the masculine contingent still at the table. "While you're doing that, we'll wash dishes for you." His sternness and scowl discouraged mutiny. "Come on, guys. We have to get this mess cleaned up before Miss Maggie can start cooking lunch."

As the others filed to the sink, Maggie crooked a finger at him.

"What is it?"

She stood on tiptoe and pulled him closer, making him wonder if she wanted another kiss before she said, "Watch the windows. I thought I saw something moving out there earlier."

"Why didn't you tell me then?"

"I figured it was just my imagination. Or the flash of a deer's white tail. I only remembered because I saw you standing over there and it worried me. If the boys really didn't do what we accused them of, there may be somebody else still roaming around out there and up to no good."

"Okay. I'm not leaving you alone in here with the Three Stooges. I'll have a look around later, after Harlan takes them off my hands."

"They really aren't all bad, you know," Maggie said as she glanced at the awkward dishwashing crew.

"They are great liars."

He didn't like it much when Maggie looked into his eyes and said, "Are you sure?"

Maggie had welcomed the arrival of the sheriff. She was sorry to see Robbie hauled off in the back of the cruiser with Luke and Will but had managed to put in a good word for him. So had Flint.

Getting rid of Elwood's remains took a little longer, particularly since his violent death required he be sent to the state crime lab in Little Rock rather than receive a cursory examination by the county coroner.

A piece of plywood nailed to the inside of her

front door kept out the cold, and a horizontal brace worked to keep it closed until she could have the whole door replaced. Blown snow beneath the body had provided enough protection to keep her porch floor clean. All it took was a few quick swipes with a broom and everything was back to normal. Almost.

She hurried inside as soon as she and Flint finished checking and feeding her animals. The fire still glowed, giving the room a cozy feel. Mark was sitting on the floor in front of a small television, watching a wildlife video, and Wolfie lay beside him.

"I think the dog is snoring," she remarked, expecting Flint to smile. He didn't. "What's wrong? I thought you'd be happy to see the boys and Elwood taken away."

"I am." He sat on the edge of the raised hearth, his back to the fire, elbows resting on bent knees.

"Is your ankle still bothering you a lot?" Constant pain would make anyone grumpy, she reasoned.

"I'll live."

"Then what's wrong? Why do you look as though your best friend just ran off with your favorite hunting dog?"

"Just have a lot on my mind, I guess."

Yeah, me, too, Maggie thought. *Important things like love and family and our future, only how do I bring that up without sounding desperate?*

"Anything I can help with?" she asked.

When Flint shook his head and stared at the floor, her mood plummeted. Was he sorry he'd kissed her? Hugged her? Acted as if he'd missed their closeness? Her heart argued for the truth behind those kisses while her brain kept planting seeds of doubt.

With a heavy sigh Flint pushed to his feet, hesitating to test his sore ankle before gingerly walking away. Every instinct in Maggie's heart insisted she follow. Temporary confusion kept her in place. Watching. Waiting for him to reveal what was bothering him so much.

"I hate to leave you for even a second, but I need to go home to clean up and change into my uniform, then drive up to headquarters and surrender my firearm to my captain until there's been an investigation of the shooting," he finally said. By that time he was pulling on his coat.

"Okay. The sheriff promised more patrols, just in case. We'll be fine."

He eyed his son. "He's a chip off the old block, isn't he? Has he always liked animals so much?"

"Ever since we adopted Wolfie when Mark was just a toddler. Before that it was fuzzy stuffed toys."

"I have a lot to catch up on, don't I?"

Was that what was getting him down? "I'm sorry," Maggie said gently as she approached to bid him goodbye. "While you're gone I'll make copies of the digital pictures my mother and I took when he was little and give you a disk to keep."

"Thanks."

Although Flint paused momentarily when he said that, he made a quarter turn away as if resisting her closeness. Maggie didn't push it. She'd give him the space he seemed to want even if it tore her apart. So much had happened in the past few weeks they both probably needed time to decompress.

"You're welcome." She clasped her hands together to keep from reaching out to him. Touching him. Offering the comfort and moral support she was certain he craved. If he'd just loosen up a little and turn back to her, maybe she'd even have a chance to hug him again.

But he did not. He didn't even raise a hand to wave as he climbed into his truck and drove away.

Maggie pressed her back to the inside of the patched door and tried to sort through her conflicting emotions. Just when she was beginning to believe she and Flint had come to a mutual understanding he'd put up a new wall.

Or was it new? she mused, empathizing with his sadness. Although she had mellowed about Flint's past choices, nothing had really changed for him in regard to their son. Mark still didn't know who his daddy was. That, she could fix. It was missing out on the boy's birth and growth that was Flint's permanent loss.

Was it a matter of forgiveness? Maggie wondered. Perhaps. Maybe his buried anger was rising to the fore now that the immediate danger to her and their son had apparently eased.

"But I can't change what's already happened," Maggie lamented aloud before closing her eyes and letting the tears flow. Once again she yearned for prayer and once again her mind failed to function adequately.

Finally, she merely whispered, "Please, Father, let Flint know I love him," then added, "And help him forgive me."

For the first time since hope had risen in her heart, it occurred to Maggie that Flint might never be able to do that.

If her impressionable five-year-old had not been close by, she might have given in to her churning, bewildering emotions and shouted at heaven in protest.

Flint knew his next task was not going to be easy. He'd fought accepting the possibility for a long time, preferring to blame the Dodd family for the attacks that Luke and the others had now denied. One thing was clear. Before he made any accusations he wanted to talk to Ira.

And if it turned out that his grandfather was guilty—or capable—of causing any of Maggie's problems, as she had hypothesized? That would probably mean the end of his and Maggie's chances for happiness together. Even if she didn't come right out and accuse him of lying to protect his kin, there would always be that nagging sense of doubt in the back of her mind.

He stomped the snow off the boot on his good leg and gently tapped the toe of the other on the mat before entering Bess's kitchen. The room was warm, welcoming him with the aroma of baking bread and taking him back to his youth. He owed these old people his life, given that he'd probably have followed in his mother's footsteps if he'd been allowed to remain poorly supervised as a youngster.

Bess was wiping her hands on her apron when she saw him. "There you are. We were worried."

"I asked the sheriff to let you know I'd be away. Didn't he tell you?"

She rolled her eyes and made a sound of disgust. "He told us, all right. I can't believe you'd take up with a woman like that. Didn't you learn your lesson years ago?"

"We all make mistakes," Flint said flatly. If she hadn't come across as so judgmental, he might not have added, "Like when you chose to marry Grandpa instead of Elwood."

"Pshaw. That was ages ago. Ira was ready for marriage and so was I. Elwood went off to fight a war in spite of me beggin' him to stay."

"Why didn't you try to make peace after he got home?"

"I was already a mama by then. What could I do? The men decided to stay mad. That was their business. It wasn't up to me to interfere."

"How about now?"

She made a face and folded her arms across her chest. "What're you talkin' about?"

Flint peered into the living room. The television was blaring, as usual, but there was no sign of Ira in his favorite recliner. "Where's Papaw?"

"Around here somewhere."

"What would be your best guess?"

"Why?"

"I need to talk to him." Sober-faced, Flint touched her elbow. "And I think you know why."

"Don't be silly."

"Where was he the night Maggie had her so-called accident?"

"Must have been here with me, like always."

Sighing, Flint nodded and withdrew. "All right. Have it your way. I'll find him myself."

Bess tried to grab his arm, but he jerked loose. "No! You leave him be, you hear. He's just a helpless old man."

"Old, yes. Helpless, no," Flint countered.

He made a brief sweep through the house without locating Ira, paused long enough to don his uniform and badge and strap on his gear so he'd have a proper holster for his sidearm until he surrendered it, then headed for the barn where the old man's truck was stored. If he couldn't find Ira, at least he could have a closer look at the pickup and see if it was damaged.

Flint fully expected to find it beneath the tarp, as before. It was his fondest hope to see no scrapes on the right front fender.

He slid the barn door wide to let in daylight. The tractor he'd been working on sat exactly where he'd left it. To its left lay the rumpled blue plastic that had been draped over Ira's truck.

The vehicle was not only missing, but there was a piece of broken frame from a headlight lying amid the straw litter.

Flint's jaw clenched. So did his fists. He now had proof who had run Maggie off the road and threatened her. What else had Ira done? Was it possible the Witherspoon boys had been telling the truth about the shootings and all the other crimes against Maggie?

He looked for tire tracks in the trampled snow outside. His already heavy breathing intensified, creating puffs of condensation in the frigid air. The signs were as plain as day. Ira hadn't driven into his own pastures to check the cattle the way he used to. He'd headed directly toward the roadway.

"Dear God," Flint said, making it into a true prayer as he ran back to his truck. Sharp pain shot from his left ankle. He refused to slow, to coddle himself.

Ira was missing. The truck was gone.

And Maggie was home alone with Mark.

NINETEEN

By the time Maggie got control of her emotions she was totally spent. She fixed PBJs for herself and Mark, then let Wolfie out the kitchen door for his afternoon constitutional.

"Is he safe?" Mark asked, watching from a window as the dog gamboled and rolled in the fresh snow. "What about wolves?"

"That was just cousin Luke playing a joke on us, remember? He said he and Will thought it was funny."

"That was mean, huh?"

Maggie nodded. "Yes, honey, that was mean."

Thoughts of the aftermath of the dog's injury led directly to Flint. She pictured him carrying her pet into the house and then… Moisture welled behind her lashes.

Maggie huffed in self-derision. "I thought I'd be out of tears by now."

She didn't realize she'd given voice to her

sentiment until Mark patted her hand. "It's okay, Mama."

"I know it is, baby. You and I will do fine, just like we always have." Dropping to one knee, she embraced him.

Mark hugged her neck before asking, "Are you still mad at Mamaw?"

Surprised by the question, Maggie hesitated. "I suppose not. She made a mistake, but she's sorry. I need to forgive her, huh?"

"Uh-huh." His arms tightened again before he released her. "Can I stay home from school some more?"

The way his young ideas jumped around made her smile. "Yes. It's a snow day. Tomorrow probably will be, too, so you can stay home."

"Hooray. Maybe the warden will come visit us later?"

That comment tore a new hole in Maggie's heart. "He came to help with Wolfie and our animals," she said. "He may not be back for quite a while."

"Yes, he will," Mark argued. "He'll come see me 'cause he's my friend. He said so." A glance toward the living room brought further comment. "Besides, he might have to shoot more bad guys."

"Whoa! Where did you get that idea?"

The child rolled his eyes as if he thought she was the naive one, not him. "Well, duh. I heard him."

She sighed heavily. "You're right. I did, too. I'm just surprised you figured it out."

Beaming, he said, "That's 'cause I'm smart."

"You certainly are. And you were very good when we had to hide again. I'm proud of you."

He flexed both biceps, arms raised. "Next time I'll punch 'em and pound 'em."

"No, you will *not*." Taking him by both shoulders, she held him still, facing her. "Understand? No fighting."

"Awww, Mama…"

"I mean it, Mark. There's been way too much fighting around here lately and I don't want to see any more. Got that?"

"Yes, ma'am."

"Good. Now, would you like to go watch another animal video while I rest a bit? Mama's really tired."

When his small hand reached to caress her cheek, he reminded her so much of his father she almost wilted.

"You can take a nap with Wolfie, like I do," he said. "I'll let him in."

It took two hands for him to turn the knob. Maggie was about to offer help when he got the door open.

Her hand flew to her mouth, covering a scream.

Ira Crawford was standing on her porch—and he had a rifle in his hand.

He sneered and stepped inside. "Where's my grandson?"

The first thing Flint saw as his truck careened down the long, slippery drive to Maggie's was multiple ruts in the snow made during and since the storm.

There was no way to tell if this was Ira's destination, but instinct warned that it might be. Confusion might have sent him another direction, of course. Was that too much to hope for?

Sliding the final corner and coming to a stop behind the house, Flint recognized the dark blue truck, and his heart lodged in his throat. The old man was here!

Wolfie's bark was coming from the direction of the animal pens. Could that mean Ira had stayed outside? Hope rose, then plummeted when Flint noticed fresh boot prints leading to the kitchen door. Not only were they too big to be Maggie's, but they were laid atop those of the dog's paws.

Flint eased himself out of his pickup and headed for the porch, careful to be quiet yet hurrying as much as possible. Ice had formed in spots where the snow had been flattened, making walking doubly treacherous.

One stair at a time, he climbed to the top and

paused to peer through the small window in the kitchen door. An open jar of jelly sat on the table. Nobody was present.

His hand closed on the knob. Tried to turn it. *Locked!*

Panic filled him. If he knocked, he might startle Ira and cause him to react. If he waited, however, it might be too late to rescue his family.

The window! The screen was off the window in Mark's room. If he hurried…

One boot slipped on ice as Flint turned. He wrenched his injured ankle. Only by the grace of God was he able to squelch a cry of pain.

Hobbling and lurching through piled snow, he peered through the first larger window he came to and was able to see Ira with Maggie. They were standing, facing each other, and he could tell she was speaking.

Mark's window was close by. Flint reached it in seconds. Tried to raise the sash. And failed.

Momentarily stunned to have his plans thwarted, he stared at the problem. Remembered how Maggie had been unable to fasten the latch because of years of overpainting. The wood was essentially glued in place, meaning he might be able to pry it loose with a blade.

A pouch on his utility belt held a knife. He pulled it out and began to cut frantically along the joint lines. The brittle paint parted on the outside and flaked away.

Flint gritted his teeth and began to pry. Did it move? He prayed he wasn't imagining things. "Please, Lord."

Moving the knife blade to a different spot at the base of the stuck sash, he pried again. And again. And again. Then he recut the side edges and tried again.

His gloves kept slipping on the hilt, so he stripped to bare hands. His knuckles were white, his muscles and joints aching, but he didn't stop trying. He couldn't. He had to get inside before it was too late.

Maggie had backed into the living room in an effort to distance herself from Ira Crawford. Mark had taken one look at a strange man standing in the doorway and had run away, much to her relief. It was her fondest hope that the child had once more headed for his hiding place in the closet.

And stayed there, she added, silently praying for her sweet little one.

It was impossible to tell what the elderly man was thinking by looking at him. When he first arrived he'd seemed furious, but now his expression was more a blank stare. She took advantage of his apparent confusion to treat him as if he were a normal visitor.

"Won't you have a seat?" Maggie made herself say, hoping she sounded a lot more welcoming than she felt.

Ira didn't answer. He merely stood in the middle of the room as if wondering where he was and how he'd gotten there.

What Maggie wanted to do was relieve him of the rifle, but she was afraid to move too fast or cause him to notice that he was armed. Instead, she reached for his opposite arm and lightly touched his elbow through his heavy jacket.

"How about sitting over here on the hearth and warming up? I love a fire on a snowy day, don't you?"

He shuffled his feet. Snow that had clung to his boots was melting and dripping onto her floor. "Can I help you off with your coat?" she asked.

Her hand traced his sleeve from elbow to cuff and she gave a tiny tug. That did it! He held out that arm and let her pull his jacket half off.

Hoping and praying the rest would go as smoothly, she let go of that sleeve and reached for the collar on his opposite shoulder, at the same time taking hold of the rifle with her other hand.

They stood there, unmoving, while Ira's rheumy glance searched hers.

Maggie didn't know what to do. Should she move? Freeze? Talk to him again? What if she let go of his coat and used both hands to try to wrest the gun from him? Suppose that was enough to snap him out of whatever fog he was in and make him fight for possession of the rifle? Suppose he won!

Just as she was about to take action, she heard a thin voice behind her. "Mama?"

No, no, no! "Go back in your special place. Now."

"But, Mama, the warden is—"

"You heard me. *Go!*"

Instead, the child hugged the back of her leg and peeked around to get a better view. Maggie didn't have to look to tell his emerald eyes were wide. They always got that way when he was interested in some new discovery.

The old man turned his head slowly. He released the rifle and shrugged out of his coat at the same time. All he said was, "Flint."

A trembling, gnarled hand reached down. "What're you doin' here, boy? You should be home with your mamaw."

Mark's confused gaze darted to his mother's face. Maggie shook her head and laid an index finger across her lips, hoping he'd understand she didn't want him to argue.

Keeping a close eye on the now unarmed old man, she managed to untangle the rifle from his coat and toss the garment aside. The rifle she kept at hand, just in case, although at this point she was beginning to doubt she'd need it.

Ira eased down onto his arthritic knees so he

was at Mark's eye level. "I've missed ya, boy. Where've you been?" Tears began to trickle down his weathered cheeks. "You got a hug for your old papaw?"

Bewildered, Mark checked with his mother.

Again, Maggie nodded. No matter what kind of person this man had once been, he was now just a lonely figure who thought he'd lost the child he'd once loved.

Although Mark was tentative about accepting a hug from a stranger and kept his worried gaze focused on his mama for moral support, he did step closer.

Ira's arms drew him in, and his thin shoulders began to shake as he clasped the boy.

To Maggie's relief and amazement, her innocent, loving son began to pat his great-great-grandfather on the back and try to comfort him.

Moreover, the child stood patiently while the old man muttered endearments, then smiled when Ira cupped his shoulders. "Your mama would be so proud."

"She is," Mark said. "She's—"

"Happy to have you here," Maggie interjected, wondering how long it would be before Ira's befuddlement cleared and he once again realized who he was. And where he was. She squelched a shiver as she tried to control her son's speech and actions via stern looks and nods.

Such methods worked best when Mark was

frightened, and unfortunately he was beginning to relax.

"I've got a new video about beavers," the boy told Ira. "Wanna watch it with me?"

Light of recognition dimmed and Ira's eyes began to glaze over as he labored to stand. Maggie saw his spine straighten and his gnarled fingers curl into fists. The instant he looked away from Mark and focused on her, his gaze seemed to radiate hate.

"You. You stole my Flint," Ira muttered, inclining his head as if trying to sort random thoughts.

"Flint left," she said.

"Liar!" Ira gestured at the boy. "I can see him plain as day. Well, you're not going to get away with it. I won't let you. I stopped you before and I can do it again."

Keeping hold of the rifle, Maggie raised her free hand. "You have this all wrong."

"You're just like all the rest, like that cheater who's tryin' to steal my farm and my woman."

Unsure whether it would help or not, Maggie tried to use the truth to draw him back to reason. "Elwood Witherspoon is dead," she said flatly.

"You think I don't know that?" Ira was shouting at her. "I shot at him myself, out in the woods. He tried to get away on one of them little scooters, but I nailed him. I know I did."

If only Flint were here to hear this confession,

Maggie thought. Then it hit her. When Mark had left his room, he tried to tell her something about the warden. What was it? What exactly had he said?

Sidling between the old man and her little boy, Maggie spoke aside to Mark. "Did you see the warden?"

"Uh-huh. By my window."

"Then I want you to open the back door."

"Now?"

"Yes."

Every time Maggie moved, Ira took a counterstep. Finally, she shoved Mark by his shoulder to get him through the doorway leading to the kitchen, then spun back to block the old man.

With both hands on the rifle she angled it across her chest, realizing immediately that she'd made an error. Holding it that way was like presenting it to its owner.

He grabbed for it. Maggie fought to hang on.

Ira gave a mighty twist and the scuffle was over. The rifle was back in his possession.

He took two steps backward and pointed it directly at her chest.

Flint was still working to free the stuck window when he heard Ira shouting. That changed everything. He bolted for the back door, ready to kick it in, and found his son standing on the porch.

"Stay here," Flint ordered, wishing he had time to stop and comfort the frightened child instead of just dashing past him. That would have to come later. Right now he had to stop his disillusioned, demented papaw from doing something unthinkable.

The sight Flint beheld when he reached Maggie's living room was a nightmare. She was shaking like a leaf, standing in front of Ira, while the old man had the barrel of a rifle so close he couldn't miss hitting her if he fired with his eyes closed.

Flint raised both hands to show he was unarmed, then spoke. "Stop, Ira. Think. You know this is wrong."

"She's a Witherspoon. She stole my grandson. I tried to steal him back, but the window was stuck shut and she tried to sic her dog on me. I have to shoot her."

"No, you don't. I'll take care of everything."

Ira glanced his way. "Who do you think *you* are?"

It occurred to Flint to try the unvarnished truth, but he could tell it wasn't the time for too many details, so he merely pointed to his badge. "I'm the law. See? You can put down the gun and leave the woman to me."

"Why should I?"

Lowering his voice and inching closer, Flint

forced a smile. "Because you know me and you know you can trust me."

"I do?"

Flint nodded. What he wanted most to do was push Maggie out of the way, but he feared any acknowledgment of her presence would refocus the old man's anger.

"That's right. You and I have shared Bess's great cooking around your kitchen table lots of times. Don't you just love her peach pie?"

"Um."

Flint didn't dare take actual steps, so he slid his feet as if he weren't approaching. Almost there. Almost close enough.

He tensed, preparing to lunge.

Movement on the other side of Ira caught his eye. *Clever, Maggie.* She had worked her way behind, away from the rifle, and cleared the way for Flint to grab it without worrying it would discharge into her.

Lifting his arm, he continued to smile. "What do you say we go see if she's made one of those pies?"

Although Ira didn't nod, he did relax enough for Flint to take the gun from him without resistance.

As he unloaded it a thin voice cheered, "Way to go!" and Flint realized that his son had watched the whole scene. That kid was smart, savvy. It wouldn't be long before he realized their genetic connection and began asking "Why?" again.

Flint would have been a lot happier about answering questions for Mark if the necessary explanation had not needed to include information about the man who had tried to kidnap him and murder his innocent mother.

Sighing, he dialed 911. It was going to be hard on everybody when he revealed Ira's crimes. Whether the old man admitted them or not, the rifle ballistics would prove who had fired at Maggie—and at him—repeatedly. Jail wasn't the answer, of course, but Ira would probably never be a free man again. His mental instability made him too dangerous.

And now that Maggie knew about Ira's attempts to end her life, there was no way she'd ever be able to forget. The old man hadn't managed to kill her, but he'd effectively killed their relationship as thoroughly as if he'd put a bullet through both their hearts.

It didn't matter what happened from here on out.

Hope had died.

TWENTY

It was quiet and dull at Maggie's after Ira and Flint left with the sheriff, giving her far too much thinking time. She considered visiting her pastor to talk about what had happened, and perhaps would, eventually. First, she'd start by visiting Faye.

To say that her mother was glad to see her was an understatement. After a moment's hesitation she grabbed Maggie and Mark in a bear hug and held on for ages. When she finally let go, her cheeks were bathed in tears.

Swiping at them, Faye apologized. "Sorry. I don't know why I'm so weepy when I should be laughing and dancing around."

"Welcome to the tissue club," Maggie said wryly. "Lately I seem to cry all the time, happy or sad."

"That's nerves, honey," her mother said. She smiled at Mark and his constant furry companion. "So, how are our boys?"

"Those two are fine." Maggie made a face. "I haven't seen hide nor hair of Flint since he arrested his own papaw."

"I heard about that from Harlan's wife, Wanda. How sad for all of them." She brightened. "At least, with the old feuding out of the way for good, you and Flint can get back together again."

"I wish." Maggie watched to make sure her son was busy playing with Wolfie before she explained. "It was as if something changed between us when he confronted Ira. He was okay with taking out Elwood, probably because it was self-defense, but handling his own kin was different. He was gentle with him and all that. He just acted odd about everything else."

"Why didn't your dog bite that nasty old man when he showed up?"

"Because he'd planned ahead, baited Wolfie, and shut him in one of the big pens in the compound. Once my watchdog was out of the way, he just came to the door. Mark opened it and the rest is history."

"But why come after you? What reason did he give?"

That question made Maggie huff. "He accused me of stealing his precious grandson, which I would love to do, by the way. Once he looked closely at Mark and saw the resemblance, he thought Mark was Flint, as a child."

"Oh, my. What did Mark do?"

Maggie smiled fondly at the memory. "He hugged Ira and patted him on the back to comfort him. If it had happened under any other circumstances, it would have been darling."

"Have you told Mark who his daddy is?"

"No. Why?"

Faye nodded. "Because he's a smart cookie. If he hasn't already put two and two together, he soon will. And when he does he's going to wonder why you and his father don't live together."

"Maybe not. Considering how many split homes and combined families there are these days, he may take it in stride."

"What about you? Are you going to accept it?"

"It doesn't matter what I want if Flint isn't interested."

"Who says he isn't?"

"He as good as told me so when he made himself so scarce. For a guy who was underfoot all the time, he's sure managed to duck me lately."

"Maybe he's waiting for you to make the first move," Faye suggested. "Let me tell you a little story."

"Now?" Maggie rolled her eyes. "I have a headache and I haven't slept well since all this started."

"Sit," Faye ordered, gesturing at the kitchen table. "I want to tell you about the man who was almost your father."

"My what?" Plunking down in one of the

kitchen chairs she rested her chin in her hands, elbows on the table.

"Your father. Perhaps someday to become your stepfather if I have my way," Faye said with a shy smile. "I was madly in love with Les Crawford when I was young. My father being a Witherspoon, my parents forbade me to date Les."

"You did what they said?"

"Absolutely. Those were different times. Most kids obeyed their parents. At least I did. Les went away just like Flint did, only we'd never had a chance to grow close, and I married Frank Morgan. End of story."

Maggie reached for her mother's hands and held them tightly. "I'm so sorry."

"It wasn't a bad marriage, although your father could be too stern at times and taught your brothers to act the same, as you well know."

"What did you mean by stepfather?"

Faye's smile became a grin. "I found Les. Called him. He's single, too, and we've met a few times, out of town of course. He's a lovely man. Mature and sweet. I didn't realize how lonely I was until I invited him back into my life."

A deep breath preceded a noisy sigh. "I'm happy for you, Mom. I really am. But what does that have to do with me and Flint?"

"Ha! I've been a doormat all my life. You're a strong-willed, sensible, modern woman and you're asking *me*?"

"I need to go find Flint, huh? Then what?"

"If you're half as self-assured as I think you are, you'll know what to do."

"I would if he was an injured raccoon," Maggie said with a nervous giggle.

Faye laughed with her. "I probably wouldn't tell him that right off."

"I won't. If he's not in the Game and Fish district office, I'll track him down. Will you watch Mark for me?"

"My pleasure. I froze some cookies I made just for him, waiting until you finally forgave me."

"That wasn't nearly as hard for me as it's going to be for Flint to get over missing out on seeing his son be born and grow."

"If he loves you, he'll forgive you."

"From your lips to God's ears." Maggie picked up her purse and headed for the door. "Feel free to pray for me. A lot."

Flint was just leaving the Mammoth Spring office when he spotted a familiar truck pulling into the lot. His spirits gave a little start, then sank like a rock in a pool of black water.

"Well, if she wants to tell me how terrible my family is, now's as good a time as any to take it," he murmured.

By the time she'd parked and gotten out of her pickup he was standing nearby. "Hi."

"Hi," Maggie said, smiling slightly and looking nervous. Flint could understand that. After all, they were going to eventually have to work out some kind of fair visitation between him and his son. Negotiations like that would make anybody edgy.

Stuffing his hands in his jacket pockets, he struck a nonchalant pose by leaning against the stone-covered front wall of the building. "Is everything all right?"

"Yes, thanks."

"You haven't had any more trouble? The boy's okay?"

"Yes, and yes," Maggie replied, "although he's bound to start asking leading questions about you and Ira soon. I've managed to distract him so far, but that trick will only work for a while."

"Understood. You're preparing for one *Why* after another?"

She chuckled under her breath and her cheeks bloomed a rosy pink. "Exactly. I plan to tell him everything appropriate for his age. It's only fair."

"Good. Keep me posted so I don't make any mistakes when I do get to visit him." To his surprise, she started to come closer. He would have backed up if he hadn't already had his back against the wall—in more ways than one.

"I've been thinking," Maggie began.

"Uh-oh."

"Don't make up your mind before you hear my ideas."

Flint wasn't convinced, particularly when she came even closer. Nevertheless, he said, "Go ahead."

She placed her hands on his shoulders, causing him to stand away from the wall. He tried to figure out what she was thinking by studying her expression, but all he was getting was what looked like joy, tempered with a tinge of fear. That made no sense at all. She had nothing more to fear. The principals of the old feud were either dead or out of commission, and any suspicions regarding Abigail Dodd's relatives had been laid to rest by Ira's full confession.

"I made a list, in my mind," Maggie said very softly. "I just can't decide what to do first."

Figuring she was planning to blame him for either not suspecting Ira soon enough or lying about it to protect him, Flint said, "Follow your instincts and you'll be fine. I can take it."

"Can you? Let's see."

There was a fresh twinkle in Maggie's blue eyes. She linked her fingers behind his neck, stood on tiptoe and pulled him closer for a kiss.

It didn't take Flint long to respond. Surprise was replaced by affection in the blink of an eye. His arms encircled her and he gave her the kind of special kiss he'd been saving for years.

When they finally came up for air he said, "Whew. If that was plan A, I can hardly wait for B."

Keeping her hands on his shoulders, she grinned and blushed. "One thing at a time. Do you still love me?"

"Is that a trick question?"

"Yes. If you say you do, you get a prize. Me."

"Then yes, I do. I thought you'd be through with me once you saw who had been trying to shoot you."

"And shoot *you*," she added. "I take it that was because he thought you were still a kid."

"From time to time he apparently did," Flint said solemnly. "At other times he knew I'd grown up, but that was when he believed I was trying to steal his farm. I suspect it was his guilt over what he'd done to Elwood years ago that brought such a thing to mind."

"It's over," Maggie said. "All of it. Behind us."

"Can we start over?" He was almost afraid to ask.

"No," she said, grinning.

Flint thought his heart was going to break before she added, "We have to pick up where we left off. Mark needs his daddy and I love you, Warden Crawford. I never stopped. I may have been mad at you when I thought you'd forgotten me, but I still loved you. With all my heart."

He would gladly have stood there for the rest of his life to listen to Maggie admitting her love.

"I never stopped loving you, either," Flint said softly as he caressed her cheek. "That was why it hurt so badly when I thought you'd had another man's child." His grin spread. "Now that I've met Mark I can see it wouldn't have mattered. I'd have loved him because he was yours."

"Well, it probably doesn't hurt that he's the image of you," she quipped. "Why don't we go pick him up and go for ice cream while we tell him who you are?"

Flint was more than thrilled. He was so overcome with peace and joy he was nearly speechless. After stealing one more kiss he took Maggie's hand and asked her, "Can we tell him his mama and daddy are finally getting married?"

"Are we ready for that?" she asked.

"I won't rush you." Flint cupped her elbow and guided her to his official vehicle. "Let's leave your truck here and take mine, for now. We have a lot to talk about. We're not the same two people who talked about getting married six years ago."

To his relief, Maggie laughed. "Mercy no. I would hope we're a whole lot smarter now. I sure am."

By the time they reached Faye's house to get Mark, there was a strange car in the driveway. Maggie delayed going inside until she'd told Flint about Les, his distant cousin who resided in Mountain Grove, Missouri, and her mother's notions about renewing their romance.

"Must be something in the water," Flint gibed. "It's a regular epidemic."

"Wait for me right here, okay? I don't want Mom to find out what we're planning for Mark and try to participate. We'll let her answer his questions later."

"Okay. Don't be long."

She leaned over to kiss him quickly and ended up lingering. That did, however, encourage her to hurry back with their son. They piled into the truck with Mark in the middle and Wolfie taking up residence in the rear passenger section among Flint's gear.

"I want vanilla with sprinkles and cookie pieces," the boy said instead of *hello*.

"That sounds good." Flint looked to Maggie. "No booster seat. Will he be safe?"

"As big as he's getting, yes," she said. "We're not going far and we can belt him in where he sits.

"We want to talk to you, honey," she said to the boy as she fastened his seat belt. "It's about your daddy."

The child's green gaze immediately rose to capture Flint's. "He's cool. I like him."

If she hadn't seen Flint's jaw drop, she might not have realized hers had, too. Recovering, she asked, "Did Mamaw tell you?"

"Naw." Mark looked very pleased with himself. "I figured it out when that grandpa guy called me his name."

"Ira is my mother's grandfather," Flint said. "I'm sorry he scared you and your mom."

"He was okay. Kinda sad," Mark offered. "Is he gonna be okay? He didn't look so good."

"He'll probably have to go into a special place to live but not jail."

"That's good. Maybe we can go visit him sometime."

Maggie swelled with pride in her son's tender heart. "Maybe we can. I think he'd like to see you again."

"Hmm. Maybe I should have chocolate instead," the boy muttered. He brightened. "Yeah. I want chocolate ice cream this time."

She looked to Flint and caught his attention. "I guess we're done talking about you being Mark's father."

"Apparently."

Maggie was so relieved she didn't know what to say or do. All her worries about how Mark would react to meeting his real father had been for nothing. The good Lord had prepared the child's heart and brought Flint into his life in a way that made the transition seamless. She was about to offer praise and thanks when Mark spoke again.

"So, when's the wedding?"

"We haven't decided yet," Maggie answered.

Both adults broke into laughter when the boy asked, "Why?"

EPILOGUE

Faye made a beautiful blushing bride. So did Maggie. They'd planned to link arms at the rear of the Serenity Chapel sanctuary and walk forward together—until Mark had wiggled between them and taken each by the hand.

"I'm gettin' a daddy," he announced proudly as he escorted his mother and grandmother to the altar.

"And a grandpa," Faye whispered aside.

He grinned from ear to ear and bellowed, "And a grandpa."

Maggie almost lost control and laughed aloud. As it was, she knew her shoulders were shaking with mirth, and if she hadn't had a bouquet to help hide her face, she figured she'd have burst into hysterics. It still might happen. She did that when she was keyed up and happy, which she certainly was.

Flint waited with Les Crawford and Pastor Malloy. They all looked handsome, but Maggie had eyes for only her groom. Despite all the times she'd imagined what her wedding would be like, she had never experienced such a rush of love and unbridled joy.

The four participants had tried to limit the number of guests, eventually giving up and issuing an open invitation via the newspaper and church bulletin. The only person Maggie knew Flint would have liked to see attend and who could not was his great-grandfather, Ira. Bess had been given a position of honor in the front row, however, and was dabbing at her eyes with a hankie.

Maggie never took her eyes off Flint from the moment she first saw him waiting for her. She hardly noticed when she and Faye reached the end of the aisle and stopped.

Pastor Malloy stepped forward with dignity and asked, "Who gives these women to be married to these men?"

Mark let go of the brides, lifted both arms into the air like a winning prizefighter and shouted, "I do!"

The ceremony came to a halt while pastor and guests, brides and grooms doubled over with laughter and blotted happy tears. It was about time.

* * * * *

Dear Reader,

Although we enter this world at birth without malice, our experiences shape us more than we imagine. And if we happen to be born into a family with secrets and prejudices, we have to fight hard to keep them from adversely affecting us. This is what happened to the Crawford and Witherspoon families. Later generations were still paying for the mistakes of a few, which is really sad—and needless. Hatred is self-destructive, as Ira and Elwood learned in this story. We can't go back and "fix" things in the past the way we would like, but we can put all that behind us and go forward, free and forgiven. This is where God and Jesus come in. The offer is open. Divine forgiveness is waiting. Our children deserve the example we set when we pardon those who have wronged us. And we deserve the joy that comes from letting go.

Whew! That was profound. Sometimes I surprise myself. I pray you will be blessed by my books and by your own life. I can be reached at PO Box 13, Glencoe, AR 72539, but a much faster reply is guaranteed if you email val@valeriehansen.com. My website is www.

valeriehansen.com, and I have a couple of Facebook pages, too. The main one is www.Facebook.com/valerie.whisenand.

Blessings,

Valerie Hansen

LARGER-PRINT BOOKS!

GET 2 FREE
LARGER-PRINT NOVELS
PLUS 2 FREE
MYSTERY GIFTS

Love Inspired®

Larger-print novels are now available...

LILP15

REQUEST YOUR FREE BOOKS!
2 FREE WHOLESOME ROMANCE NOVELS
IN LARGER PRINT
PLUS 2
FREE
MYSTERY GIFTS

✻✻✻✻✻✻✻✻✻✻✻✻✻✻✻✻✻✻✻✻✻✻

HEARTWARMING™

❦❦❦❦❦❦❦❦❦❦❦❦❦❦❦❦❦❦❦❦❦❦

Wholesome, tender romances

YES! Please send me 2 FREE Harlequin® Heartwarming Larger-Print novels and my 2 FREE mystery gifts (gifts worth about $10). After receiving them, if I don't wish to receive any more books, I can return the shipping statement marked "cancel." If I don't cancel, I will receive 4 brand-new larger-print novels every month and be billed just $5.24 per book in the U.S. or $5.99 per book in Canada. That's a savings of at least 19% off the cover price. It's quite a bargain! Shipping and handling is just 50¢ per book in the U.S. and 75¢ per book in Canada.* I understand that accepting the 2 free books and gifts places me under no obligation to buy anything. I can always return a shipment and cancel at any time. Even if I never buy another book, the two free books and gifts are mine to keep forever.

161/361 IDN GHX2

Name _____ (PLEASE PRINT) _____

Address _____ Apt. # _____

City _____ State/Prov. _____ Zip/Postal Code _____

Signature (if under 18, a parent or guardian must sign) _____

Mail to the **Reader Service:**
IN U.S.A.: P.O. Box 1867, Buffalo, NY 14240-1867
IN CANADA: P.O. Box 609, Fort Erie, Ontario L2A 5X3

* Terms and prices subject to change without notice. Prices do not include applicable taxes. Sales tax applicable in N.Y. Canadian residents will be charged applicable taxes. Offer not valid in Quebec. This offer is limited to one order per household. Not valid for current subscribers to Harlequin Heartwarming larger-print books. All orders subject to credit approval. Credit or debit balances in a customer's account(s) may be offset by any other outstanding balance owed by or to the customer. Please allow 4 to 6 weeks for delivery. Offer available while quantities last.

Your Privacy—The Reader Service is committed to protecting your privacy. Our Privacy Policy is available online at www.ReaderService.com or upon request from the Reader Service.

We make a portion of our mailing list available to reputable third parties that offer products we believe may interest you. If you prefer that we not exchange your name with third parties, or if you wish to clarify or modify your communication preferences, please visit us at www.ReaderService.com/consumerschoice or write to us at Reader Service Preference Service, P.O. Box 9062, Buffalo, NY 14240-9062. Include your complete name and address.

YES! Please send me **The Western Promises Collection** in Larger Print. This collection begins with 3 FREE books and 2 FREE gifts (gifts valued at approx. $14.00 retail) in the first shipment, along with the other first 4 books from the collection! If I do not cancel, I will receive 8 monthly shipments until I have the entire 51-book Western Promises collection. I will receive 2 or 3 FREE books in each shipment and I will pay just $4.99 US/ $5.89 CDN for each of the other four books in each shipment, plus $2.99 for shipping and handling per shipment. *If I decide to keep the entire collection, I'll have paid for only 32 books, because 19 books are FREE! I understand that accepting the 3 free books and gifts places me under no obligation to buy anything. I can always return a shipment and cancel at any time. My free books and gifts are mine to keep no matter what I decide.

272 HCN 3070 472 HCN 3070

Name	(PLEASE PRINT)	
Address		Apt. #
City	State/Prov.	Zip/Postal Code

Signature (if under 18, a parent or guardian must sign)

Mail to the **Reader Service:**
IN U.S.A.: P.O. Box 1867, Buffalo, NY 14240-1867
IN CANADA: P.O. Box 609, Fort Erie, Ontario L2A 5X3

* Terms and prices subject to change without notice. Prices do not include applicable taxes. Sales tax applicable in N.Y. Canadian residents will be charged applicable taxes. This offer is limited to one order per household. All orders subject to approval. Credit or debit balances in a customer's account(s) may be offset by any other outstanding balance owed by or to the customer. Please allow 4 to 6 weeks for delivery. Offer available while quantities last. Offer not available to Quebec residents.